PAULINE'S

DIARY

An abusive journey of a young woman

BEN DARKWA

i

BEN DARKWA

TABLE OF CONTENTS

CHAPTER 1

Her back was hunched and she shook with every breath she took. Her face was stained with tears and she could not help but let them keep gushing out. Thirty-two-year-old Joyce was well-dressed with a scarf around her neck. Her long gown looked untidy like she had put it on in a hurry. Her dark glasses, however, prevented anyone who dared to look at her from seeing the tears and how red her eyes were. Not that anyone had spared her a look; the park was quiet at such hours in the day. The main reason she had come there was to get some fresh air and have some time to think.

Pauline scrolled down her phone as the heels of her pumps smacked the ground. She was professionally dressed in a grey suit and carried a briefcase. She was late for work, but she needed the walk through the park. From the corner of her eyes, she caught a woman on a bench. She spared her a glance and continued walking, then stopped. Wasn't that Joyce? She took another look and nodded. Yes, she was the one. Joyce was a patient from the psychiatric unit she used to attend weekly. The older woman heaved as she cried, and twenty-nine-year-old Pauline moved towards her, worried.

She sat next to her on the bench, and Joyce quickly looked up. Even with the glasses covering her eyes, it was obvious that she had been crying. The smile she flashed Pauline was very fake.

"Long time no see, Joyce, how have you been? What's wrong?" Pauline asked.

As Joyce removed her glasses and the scarf which covered her neck, Pauline's blood grew hotter. Her left eye was heavily bruised and her neck area was red.

"What happened to you?" Pauline asked, worried. "Who did this to you?"

"My husband," Joyce confessed.

"Your husband?"

Joyce nodded. "He's the one, as usual. I have been abused by him sexually and psychologically for as long as I can remember, and although I have lived with this, the rate at which he has turned me into his punching bag is alarming." She burst into tears and Pauline wrapped her arms around her, holding her close, comforting her.

"Have you reported this to the police?" Pauline asked, as her sobs began to die down.

Joyce shook her head.

"Why haven't you done so? Domestic violence's not a thing to be taken lightly. Apart from the physical damage it does to its victims, it leads to isolation from friends. It also causes depression, which can lead to dementia and other mental health issues. It also affects the working performance of its victims."

"I..."

"When did you see me last at the psychiatric unit asking for help?" Pauline asked. Joyce shook her head and Pauline went on. "I'm free from the crisis I was going through as a result of the help I received in addition to my force of will to change my destiny. You need to report this to the police as soon as possible."

Joyce shook her head. "I can't do that. He threatened me. He told me he would divorce me and will leave me with no financial support. I lost my job and don't have any means of survival. I will be left with nothing. Nothing, Pauline. How can I survive in this economy?" Joyce asked as tears began to pool in her eyes.

Pauline patted her back in comfort. "Joyce, just because you're scared of the future doesn't mean you have to endure this torture you're going through. I can help you through this, so don't be scared. You know, I have been through what you're going through. But I overcame it. Yes, it is now a thing of the past, but for so long I was haunted."

"Really?" Joyce asked.

"Yes, perhaps even far worse than what's happening with you," Pauline said with a sad smile.

"What happened?" Joyce asked curiously.

"It started when I was a child…"

"Daddy, stop! Daddy, please stop!" ten-year-old Pauline cried. She tried to push her small body between her father and her mum, who was being beaten, but to no avail. There was no way to stop her father, who was so angry that he could not listen to a word of reason. "Daddy, please," she continued to cry, as her father, Mr. Griphix, rained blows on his wife, Fatima.

"Useless woman. Good for nothing human being," her father yelled as he continued to beat her mother.

Tears ran down her mother's face as he continued to beat her while she cried for him to stop. Then, he stopped. He pushed her to the ground and walked out of the room, insulting her.

Pauline quickly ran to her mother who quivered as she took fast breaths. Her face was bruised and blood oozed from her nose. "Mummy," Pauline cried, hugging her mother. Seeing her mother in such a state made her scared and worried. She had seen this play out several times and was tired of it. She just wanted it to end and for her father never to beat her mother again.

In an instant, her father returned to the room, this time with a belt. His face fumed with anger as he approached his wife.

"Daddy, no!" Pauline cried, shaking her head. As he raised the belt, she tried to cover her mother from her father's rage with her little body. She let out a scream as the belt touched her.

"See what you have done!" her father yelled at her mother. He wrestled Pauline away from her mother and pushed her into a corner. His attention returned to her mother as he flogged her with the belt. Both females cried out, the older from the pain inflicted on her and the younger with the emotional pain she felt watching her father beat her mother. It was a pain that would follow her through childhood and would shape her life as an adult.

CHAPTER 2

The rain continued to pour down heavily with great vengeance. It was mixed with thunder and lightning, which showed the wrath of the rain. It was a cold day and anyone caught outside would surely regret it and wish for comfort. It had been raining for several hours and at three in the morning, it showed no sign of stopping.

Pauline lay in a warm, big, comfortable bed away from the cold outside. But even though she was not out in the rain, a storm was brewing within her. She was restless as she turned from one side to another. Her body was covered in sweat even though the atmosphere was cold. Suddenly, she jolted out of bed screaming, "Daddy, stop!"

Her husband, Robert, woke up by her side. He groaned as he stared at her. "What the hell is wrong with you?" he asked furiously, glaring at her.

The only answer that he got was the tears that flowed down Pauline's cheeks in silence. He groaned again, this time with disgust. He shook his head and lay back on the bed, covering himself with the blanket. In a few seconds, his snores filled the room.

Pauline remained in her sitting position, shivering for a few seconds, trying to get herself together, but it was an ordeal. She had been through this several times in her life, and they seemed to worsen after she had a fight with her husband. She managed to get up from the bed with shaky legs and went to the bathroom. She closed the door behind her and put on the light. She walked to the mirror and stared at herself. She looked terrible. Her hair was pasted to her head with sweat and her eyes were red from stress and tiredness. She turned on the tap and cold water rushed out. She washed her face and although it did not make much difference, at least she looked better.

Take a deep breath, she told herself it was only a dream. She closed her eyes and took short, deep breaths, in and out, as she tried to calm herself down. Everything is going to be alright, she silently told herself. It was just a nightmare, nothing more.

Robert sat up on the bed and turned to his side to find it empty. He saw the bathroom light on and shook his head. He sat further up on the bed and reached for his phone, which was on the bedside table. He typed in his password and went to his WhatsApp messaging application. He smiled as he read a new message. It was a picture of Selina, half-naked and smiling at him. He was glad to see that she was online.

"I can't stop missing you, sweet," he typed.

Selina: "You dare not."

Robert smiled and sent a message back, "Why?"

Selina: "Once tasted, always available in your mind."

"Hmmm… Bad girl."

Selina: "Why are you even awake? You know you have work tomorrow."

Robert rolled his eyes. "She had some stupid nightmare and woke me up."

Selina: "Sorry about that; you know you wouldn't have that around me."

He smiled; that was true. Nights spent with Selina were always full of fun all through the night, not like the ones he had to spend with his wife. His eyes quickly went to the door when he heard the bathroom light switch flick off. He quickly shut off his phone and jumped back on the bed, closing his eyes and pretending to sleep, snoring as an additional effect.

Feeling much better, Pauline headed back to the room to join her husband on the bed, his loud snores filling the room. She went to the fridge first and grabbed a bottle of water, which she finished in a few gulps. That was the crazy thing about the nightmares: whenever she woke up, she was always thirsty. She moved to the bed and lay next to her husband.

She stared at him and tapped him after a few seconds of making a decision. He gave no response. She tapped him again but got no response again. However, he got up finally and glared at her.

"What is it?" he yelled.

Tears pooled in her eyes at the anger in his voice.

"Can't you talk, woman? Can't you see the time? You think I don't need to rest for tomorrow, huh?"

"Sorry…" Pauline said, averting her eyes.

"Sorry for yourself," Robert said with a glare. He pushed the blanket closer to him and fell back to the bed.

Pauline remained in her position then dropped to her side of the bed. She knew better than to reach for him again. He was in an angry mood already, who knew what else he could do in such a state.

*

Twenty-four-year-old Vivian hummed as she ironed her first cousin Robert's shirt. The earplugs in her ears were attached to her phone in her back pocket. She shook her waist as she moved to the beat of the song. The music soon stopped when a phone call came in. She let go of the iron and pulled the phone out of her pocket.

She grimaced as she stared at the caller; it was Thomas, her boyfriend, or better yet, her ex-boyfriend. She had no idea how to classify their relationship anymore. She wanted to ignore his call, but she knew him, and he would keep on calling until she answered.

"What is it?" she asked. After she heard him speak for a little while, she shouted at him. "Thomas, will you shut the hell up and listen to me?"

"Please don't yell at me, I am not deaf," Thomas said in a soft voice, unlike his normal voice.

"Don't even try me, Thomas. It may be morning, but I will start with you. I don't know why we're discussing this. I'm not giving in on this. What do you take me for, eh?"

"Come on, Vivi. Just shush for a second."

Vivian shouted again. "Don't you dare tell me to shush. Do I look like a dog to you? It seems you have no respect for me anymore."

A bang on the door startled her, but she quickly ended the call and the music continued. She nodded her head and shook her hips to the beat of the song and continued to iron the shirt. When the door opened, Robert stepped into the laundry room where Vivian ironed. He was freshly clean and had droplets of water still in his hair. He was in a white singlet and blue jeans which he was fastening with a belt. In his other hand, he carried a pair of shoes.

He watched Vivian for a while and she went on, pretending that she had not seen him. "Vivian," he called. She ignored him and continued singing and dancing. "Vivian!" he called again.

Vivian dropped the earphones and turned around. "Yes, cousin?"

"Who was that?" he asked.

"Huh?"

He gave her a condescending look like she thought him stupid to fall for her little drama. "It was Thomas, wasn't it?"

Vivian nodded. She knew there was no need to deny it. He could just check her phone records if she denied it.

Robert shook his head. "That guy is not good for you. I have told you this countless times, but you're just too stubborn to listen to me. You two are just not compatible. You're, well, not an angel, but he's a demon. Let whatever you have be over. Let it go! Let me tell you something that you may not know: real men don't go to prison. Are you hearing me?" he asked, pulling his ear.

"Cuz, I am trying very hard. But I think he has changed." She nodded in affirmation. "Everyone deserves a chance; don't you think?" she stopped when she saw the glare on his face.

"What are you saying?" Robert snapped. "That useless boy has been to prison. Do you know what that means? He's a disgrace to everyone who knows him. Do you know that it is a big disgrace to this family for you to date someone like that? Let me tell you something: if I catch that boy within a 5-mile radius of this house, I will take matters into my own hands. If you like, don't listen to me, continue to fool yourself around that non-entity." He glared at her one last time, then angrily left and went back into the house.

Vivian sighed. This was the type of trouble she was trying to avoid with Thomas. She turned back to the ironing table.

*

Pauline quietly set the table, sparing the TV a glance once in a while. Her nightgown reached down to her knees, a hair net covered her hair, and she wore bathroom slippers. She had yet to take a bath, as the first thing she had done when she got up was to make breakfast for her husband, just the way he liked it. Although Vivian was the house caretaker, something Pauline had chosen to do was to prepare her husband's meals. That was something she could not leave to someone else to do. Every meal she made, she prepared with love.

She looked up when he came in from the laundry room where she knew Vivian had to be ironing his shirt like she did most mornings. He went to a couch and sat down then began to put on his socks and shoes. By his side was a small bag which he usually took for his weekend trips. Her brow lifted as she noticed it; he had not told her he was leaving for a trip.

"Honey, breakfast is ready," Pauline called.

Robert's Samsung Galaxy vibrated as it rang. He turned the phone around. It was Selina calling. "Not interested," he snapped at her.

Pauline's lips tightened into a firm line. Then she moved quietly towards him. As she sat down beside him, he quickly snatched his phone out of her reach, even though she had not been interested in it.

"Rob," Pauline said.

He looked up at her from his shoes. "What?"

Pauline sighed. "You do realize you're hurting me? You're killing me, Rob. I am dying inside. What have I done wrong to you? In what way have I wronged you, my love? Please tell me so I can make amends."

"Look, I don't have time for this," Robert said.

"Please, Robert, tell me. At least let me know where I have erred so that I can make amends. Please, Robert, I beg you."

"I hate your—"

They were interrupted by Vivian, who had just entered the living room, bringing his shirt with her. Robert nodded at her in appreciation and put on the shirt. He nodded at his bag and she took it outside to the car.

"Robert, please…" Pauline was cut short by his phone vibrating. She saw the gaze he threw at the phone, then back at her as if she was an obstacle to him answering the call. "Do you want me to excuse you answering the call?" she asked.

Robert shot her a glare. "It's my phone, not yours. Don't I have the right to pick up my calls when I want to and when I don't want to?"

He put on his jacket and grabbed his briefcase by his side. He reached for a stool and picked up a bottle of water, his phone charger, and his wallet. He walked to the door without a word to his wife or even a look back.

"Rob!" Pauline called after him.

Robert sighed as he stopped at the door. "What is it?"

"What will you have for dinner? Should I make your favourite tonight?" she asked, a smile creeping on her face. She knew how much he loved it.

He turned around and looked at her with pity. "Pauline, you better take your drugs on time. It's getting worse day by day and there's only so much I can take."

"What do you mean?" Pauline asked confused.

"Damn!" he cursed. "This is driving me crazy. I can't lie to you. I get mad when you keep forgetting things. Stop missing out on your drugs, for Christ's sake!"

Pauline's face fell and she reached for the couch which she dropped down onto. "But you didn't tell me anything about this, Rob. I would have remembered. You didn't tell me you were travelling."

"Well, I did, and it is not my fault that you keep forgetting whatever I tell you every second."

"At least tell me where you're going to. Please," Pauline added.

He shook his head in pity and dismay. "When I tell you to keep taking your drugs, you won't listen. You feel you know everything. Okay, then, since you don't want to listen to me, I won't repeat myself now or ever. You need to learn to obey me. When you see me, you see me."

He walked out the door and slammed it hard behind him, startling Pauline. At that moment, she was thrown back to the past. She could remember an incident that happened when she was ten years old.

She was at the dining table eating cereal. Her eyes were, however, not on her plate, but on her mum who was in tears. She was in her night dress and held a tray holding a hot meal made for Pauline's father. Her father, however, walked past them. Already dressed for work, he picked up his briefcase and walked out the door without a word, shutting the door hard behind him, startling Pauline and her mother. This he did several times. He knew she woke up early to prepare his meals, but he never took the time to appreciate or eat them, making her mother weep out of frustration.

A teardrop fell down from Pauline's eyes and she could not help the flood that came rushing down a second later.

*

Vivian jumped up, startled when she heard the bang of the door. She quickly removed the earplugs from her ear and dropped the rag she had been using to clean her cousin's car. "God! Don't tell me those people are fighting again," she muttered, shaking her head, still frightened.

She could tell it had been something of that nature when she saw her cousin approach her from the porch with anger on his face.

"Open the gate!" he shouted.

She didn't wait for him to repeat his instruction and ran to open the gate. Robert got into the jeep and drove it to the opened gate. He drove out a little and the window rolled down. He crooked his fingers at Vivian, signalling for her to come to him.

"Cousin," she said, when she hurried to him.

"Make sure she takes all her drugs," he said.

Vivian frowned then nodded. "I will."

"And don't disrespect her. Just because you're my cousin does not mean you can treat her the way I do. Are you hearing me?"

"Yes."

"Good. Make sure she takes those drugs. If she doesn't, you know I will know. And I will hold you responsible. I don't want to hear any excuses. You're in charge while I am gone. I'm going on a business trip, and I don't know when I am coming back, but don't expect me for some time. I left money in the usual place for anything you need in the house. Make sure you take care of the home well in my absence," Robert continued.

Vivian nodded. "Thank you, I will make sure I do everything you said. Um… my mum is in the hospital."

"What happened?" Robert asked with concern.

"They said her blood pressure went up and they had to take her to the hospital. They did a test and they said she has malaria as well. I might have to go and see her if they don't discharge her on time."

"Better than the alternative; not that I want her to be sick because of that. I was thinking that your useless father might have had a hand in this. Even though I am sure he was the one to surge her blood pressure. I just hope he has not beaten my aunt again."

Vivian scratched her chin. "I don't know, sha. But I won't be surprised. But Cousin, with all due respect, you're no different."

Robert jolted and glared at her. "What are you saying?"

"I'm…"

"You should know when to keep your mouth shut, stupid girl. I hope you know who you're talking to. Don't forget that you're under my roof!" He was interrupted from his scolding by the ringing of his phone. He looked down at the phone. It was Selina. He knew she must have been waiting a while for him. It was time to hit the roads and meet up with her. "Anyway, I have to go now, I have an important meeting I need to attend. Make sure you keep me posted. And don't do anything stupid in my absence. You know who I am talking about."

He drove off and answered the call with a smile. Vivian watched him zoom off, then plugged in her earplugs. She closed the gates and headed back to the house. She paused as her phone rang. It was Thomas.

"Thomas, what is it?" she asked, annoyed.

"Come on, Vivi," he said.

"Do you have a death wish?" she asked again.

"Baby, don't be annoyed, but you cut the call on me before. You know I don't like it."

"My cousin came into the room, and he knew you were the one who called. You should have seen the way he was angry with me!"

"Calm down, Vivi. It's just that I need that document badly. Please, I need it for a job application," Thomas said.

Vivian scoffed. "That's your loss because you're not getting it."

"Vivi, baby. Please listen to me, darling. You know I love you very much. If I get this job, it will make us happy forever and ever. I promise you this, so just help me with it.

"Ha! You're not serious. Talk to the hand, because the ear is not listening."

"Vivi, baby, please help me," Thomas pleaded.

"Look, don't disturb me again, Thomas. I have a mad woman in the house who needs to take her drugs. The last thing I need is your drama. Just leave me alone." She cut the call off before he could plead anymore. She headed back to the house, singing.

CHAPTER 3

Pauline slowly ate the meal she had prepared for her husband. She wasn't ready to eat, but it was better than letting the food and the time she had invested go to waste. She had cleaned off the tears from her face and composed herself. She wasn't going to let what happened get to her.

Vivian got to the living room with the clothes she had packed from the washline and took them to the bedroom. She returned, this time with Pauline's drugs. "Ma, it is time to take your drugs." She stopped when she saw that the plate was almost full. Pauline had barely eaten anything. "Ah! You know you can't take your drugs without eating. You need to eat well before you take your drugs so that your energy level will be up."

Pauline nodded and pushed more food into her mouth, but after a few minutes more, she shoved the plate away from her. She had lost her appetite. Vivian knew she wasn't going to eat anymore. She went to the kitchen and returned with a jug of water and a glass which she poured the water into. She reached for the bag of drugs and began to sort them out.

"Vivian," Pauline said.

"Yes?" Vivian said, looking up for a second.

"Can I ask you a question?"

"Sure. But see, time's going fast, and your situation might get worse. You need to take your drugs now because if it gets worse, Robert will hold me responsible and I will be in trouble."

Pauline ignored her and said again, "Can I ask you a question?"

Vivian sighed. "Yes."

"Am I crazy?" Pauline asked. "I'm a hardworking woman. I have everything I need at my disposal. So why then does your cousin treat me this way?"

"Pauline, consider yourself a lucky woman. It is not easy to have a handsome, strong husband with good standing in our society. You got a good catch with Cousin Robert. You don't think there are many women out there who want to be in your condition? Me, I am looking for a man like that. Instead, I am here in your house playing maid because of my good for nothing ex-convict boyfriend who my family is trying to protect me from. You think if I see a man like Cousin Robert, I won't follow him and move into his house? Any woman would do so. Getting beat up once in a while by your husband is a normal thing. Ask anybody and they will tell you so. Even my mummy, my dad beats her once in a while, and she hasn't died. For as long as I can remember it has been happening. At times she might go to the hospital, but she remains strong over the years. You know us women with our big mouths. Once in a while, we need a small beating to reset our brain. It is either he beats you or you be the strong one and beat him up. You're a good size, all you'd have to do is sit on him." Vivian shook her head and burst into a laugh at her joke.

Pauline sighed. "I guess you're right. Men will always be men. They will always have the upper hand no matter what. Besides, they are the stronger sex. What am I even complaining about?"

Vivian nodded in agreement. "Exactly! You should be happy he comes home at night and that he cares for you. There's this woman who my mum buys from in the market. The husband beats her every single day. If you see this woman, you just know, always one scar or another on her face. Her face is very rough, as well as her body. She even looks very old, and when I heard her age, I was very shocked that she was that young. Her husband is also a drunkard and chases anything in skirts. But it's her own luck. She knows she can't leave him. Who will be her husband? Where will she find a man at her age? Who will be a father to her children? It is better for you to be with the demon you know than the angel you don't know. What about my cousin's friend. You know Yvonne right? A friend of hers gave birth to three girls and no boy. Doctors warned her not to get pregnant again as her body had gone through a lot. It was then the husband began to beat her. Her in-laws called her names since she couldn't give birth to a boy. Her husband, a very educated man, continued to beat her every day that her womb was filled with girl children. This woman was very pretty, even contested in beauty pageants when she was in university…"

"What happened?" Pauline asked. She wondered why the woman would be blamed for this when it was the man who was supposed to produce the chromosome which produced male children.

"The husband could not take it anymore and pushed her out of the house. Her family had to go and beg him to take her back. People warned her, but she still got pregnant. She and the little girl she gave birth to died. Do you know the husband remarried a month later? The woman was already pregnant. Guess what child she gave birth to."

"Girls?" Pauline asked.

Vivian laughed, shaking her head. "Yes, and twins, for that matter. The next child was another girl. This one, too, he's beating her to give him a male child." She finished sorting the drugs which Pauline was supposed to take in the morning. "Let's take the drugs now, ma. So that we won't have problems with Cousin Robert."

Pauline nodded and stretched her palm forward. Vivian placed the drugs in Pauline's hand and she threw them into her mouth before taking a gulp of water. She did this two more times before she was done with her morning round.

Vivian got up and left her to finish the rest of her breakfast.

*

After a small dinner and taking her drugs, Pauline fell asleep on a couch in the living room. It was the first time in a while she felt she could sleep well, and she hoped she would not have to wake up to one of her nightmares.

31

In the kitchen, with her headphones attached to her head, as usual, Vivian washed the night's dinner plates. She hummed in addition, singing at intervals off-key to the song she was listening to. The loud song made her unaware of the thud outside the house. She had no idea about the intruder who had climbed the fence and had jumped over it. She had no idea that someone else was now in the compound with her and Pauline.

The intruder quietly made his way around the corner of the house. He stopped by the kitchen window and quickly ducked when Vivian looked his way. He was dressed in black, his face masked and his hands in black gloves.

Vivian danced as she went to the window where the plate rack was placed. She giggled as she sang a song she had just composed. "Pauline's deeply asleep. Very fast asleep. Only a slap can wake her up from her slumber. The world keeps asking if she's okay." She laughed and shook her head. Done with the dishes, she wiped her hands clean and hummed as she left the kitchen. She stopped then switched off the kitchen light before heading out.

Waiting for her steps to be far away, the intruder slipped a key into the door's keyhole. Slowly and silently, he opened the back door which led into the kitchen. He stepped in, looking around intensely to see if he was alone or not. He closed the door behind him and moved further into the kitchen. He listened carefully to make sure that no one was within his reach. Then he tiptoed out of the kitchen. He passed through the kitchen and into the dining room. His eyes caught Pauline, who lay on a couch sleeping. His hand went immediately to a gun by his side. He brought it forward as though he intended to shoot her, but stopped himself.

He immediately stepped back into the darkness and hid under the dining table when he heard Vivian come back to the living room area. She passed his hiding spot and went to the parlour light and turned it off. Leaving Pauline alone in the darkness, she turned around and went down the hall and into her room.

The intruder quickly went to Pauline and positioned himself at the foot of the sofa. He pulled the gun from his side and pointed it at Pauline's head. Oblivious to what was happening, Pauline remained asleep. With a huff, the intruder hit the sofa, hard. Pauline, however, remained asleep. He had to hit the sofa two more times before her eyes opened.

She looked up from her position and stared at the masked man in fear. He lifted his gloved fingers to his mouth, signalling for to her to keep quiet. "Shhh…"

Her eyes widened in terror. She opened her mouth to scream, but the cocking of the trigger silenced her. He shook his head and motioned at the gun. Pauline understood him perfectly well: if she screamed or caused trouble, he was going to kill her.

"Where's your husband?" he asked.

Pauline froze in hesitation. She looked towards the hallway door which was closed and back at him.

"Don't even think of screaming," he said. "I will shoot you right here and you will die instantly. I am not here to play games. Listen to me carefully, because I will not repeat myself. Do you understand?"

Pauline nodded as she waited for his instructions.

"Good. You must obey all my instructions and answer all my questions accurately, I will know when you're lying and will not hesitate to kill you. Now I will ask you one more time, where is Robert?"

"He… he… left this morning. He did not… tell me where he was going," Pauline managed to muster out in fear.

He looked at her intensely and she could see his cold eyes reading her soul to tell if she was lying or not. Her heart skipped a beat. What if he thought wrong, that she was lying, and killed her?

"Get up slowly and lead me to his room," the intruder said, calming her for an instant and convincing her that he believed her. Fear set in, though, as she wondered why he wanted her to take him to their room. She stared at him blankly and he waved the gun at her.

She did as he had instructed and slowly got up from the couch. He grabbed her hand forcefully and pushed her towards the hallway. As they passed Vivian's room, she wanted to scream for help. But she knew doing so would not only hurt her, but also Vivian. It was best to cooperate with the man.

She stopped in front of her and her husband's room and opened the door. Immediately after they got in, he locked the door. It was then she noticed he was holding a bottle with a substance inside it. She gulped as she wondered what was in it. He pushed her towards the bed. "Sit down there, and don't say a word or do anything stupid. Don't play with me, woman, because I will kill you."

Pauline nodded obediently and sat down on the bed. He dropped the bottle and the gun by the window. She was surprised when he pulled their wardrobe open and began to look for something. She had no idea what it could be. He moved to the drawers then searched every area of the room. His eyes were fixed on her and she sat frozen unable to do a thing or say a word as he invaded her privacy.

There was a knock at the door and both of them turned. It was Vivian. "Pauline, open the door! Why did you lock the door?" she asked, pounding furiously. She knocked harder when Pauline gave no answer. "Open this door! Do you want Cousin Robert to be angry with me? You crazy woman, open the door!"

Noticing his attention on the door, Pauline reached for the house phone. From the corner of his eye, though, the intruder spotted her. He jumped on her and quickly grabbed the phone from her hand. Pauline was shocked when he slapped her hard with the back of his palm. She stared at him, dazed. She touched her face and her eyes widened as she felt blood come out from her nose. In fear, she scurried out of bed to the ground. Tears began to pool in her eyes. She did not want to die, at least not now, in her prime, and at the hands of someone else.

"Don't you dare say a word!" he whispered. He picked up the gun from the window sill and waved it at her. "I warned you, didn't I? I told you not to try anything stupid. I should kill you."

"Please," Pauline begged, shaking her head. "I'm sorry." She closed her eyes and prayed quietly. God, please, don't let him kill me. God, please save me.

"Do you know Janet? Janet Cole?" the intruder asked.

Pauline's eyes came open in confusion.

"Do you know Janet Cole?" he asked again, this time louder.

Pauline nodded. "Yes… I do. She died a couple of weeks ago, didn't she? She committed suicide I think." Pauline nodded again. "Yes, she killed herself."

Even with the mask on, she could feel the fury on his face. His hand clenched tighter around the gun's barrel. "How did you know her?" he asked.

"I met her a couple of times. Rob introduced her to me," Pauline said. She remembered the young woman, who always wore a smile, that had said she knew something which Pauline didn't know. A confident and satisfied smile which seemed to mock her, but which Pauline always disregarded, telling herself that it was all in her head.

"He should have told you how she really died," the intruder muttered before turning his back on her. He crouched by the bed and placed his hand under it looking for something. Placing the gun on the window, he used both hands to pull a wooden box from beneath the bed. It was locked with a padlock and had the inscription, 'Private.' He scoffed and pulled a dagger from the bag he had with him. With a few hits of the dagger, the padlock was broken.

Pauline stared at the box curiously. She had no idea such a thing was even in the house. Her eyes quickly went to the door as Vivian continued knocking hard and calling her names. "Open this door! Why are you being stupid? If Cousin Robert does anything to me, I will make sure I deal with you!"

Pauline could hear her phone ringing in the living room. Vivian went silent and her footsteps could be heard leaving the door.

Vivian returned with the ringing phone to the door. She was sweating out of frustration and angry at the same time. Her hair was scattered and her earpiece was on the ground. She could not understand why the crazy woman had locked herself in the room. One moment she had been dead asleep in the living room and the next she was locked up in her bedroom. She wondered what kind of trouble she had gotten herself into with her cousin. All because of his lunatic of a wife. Worst of all was that she could hear strange noises coming from the room as if Pauline was throwing things around. This mad woman better not give me work to do, she thought.

She pulled a hair clip from her hair and put it in the door hole. She had seen this method of opening doors with hair clips in movies so it couldn't be that hard, could it? But after a few tries, she realized there was no way she could do such a thing. She slid to the floor tired, her back against the door.

CHAPTER 4

The room was in disarray as a result of the frantic search by the intruder. Even after taking things from the wooden box, he had continued to look around, throwing things everywhere.

Both of them then turned their attention to the landline in the room, which was now ringing. He went straight to it and cut the phone line with the dagger. Pauline stared at him in fear as he quickly reached for her. She struggled against him; she was not going to go down without a fight. He, however, held her firmly and pulled a cloth out of his pocket that he used to cover her mouth. Then he put her hands together and tied them.

Pauline watched him, scared. He reached for one of her handbags and removed the contents of the wooden box, putting them into the bag. Pauline panicked when, in a swift move, he stabbed the centre of a table with the dagger. "A gift for Robert," he said. He opened the window and jumped out of it.

Relieved, Pauline took a deep sigh. She was not going to die. Thank you, God, Pauline thought. She had survived that ordeal and was still alive.

The intruder ran to the fence and jumped over it, the same way he had gotten into the compound. He got into the driver's seat of a dark car and quickly started the engine. The car came alive and he zoomed off. He placed the bag on the front seat and removed the mask from his face. He drove until he was out of the street. He, however, slowed down as he approached a police night barrier. He removed the bag from the passenger seat and threw it to the ground of the back seat, putting it out of sight.

He rolled down his window and smiled in greeting at the police officer. "Officer, good evening," he said.

The officer nodded back in greeting. "Where's your driving license and car documents?" he asked.

The man reached for the dashboard and brought out an envelope which he handed to the officer. The officer looked through them and then at him and said, "Simon?"

"Yes, officer," he answered.

He handed them back to him and waved at his colleague at the barrier to let him go. Simon nodded and drove slowly past the barrier before he sped off. He drove for a few minutes and suddenly a noise came from his car engine.

"Not now!" Simon muttered, but the car came to a halt. "Damn!" he cursed. He sat there for a few seconds, then huffed in frustration. He opened the door and stepped out of the car. He opened the bonnet to check what the fault was. He shook his head as he continued to check the engine. A rustle in the bush nearby made him raise his head. He quickly reached for his gun by his side, but it was not there.

He sighed in relief when he saw a hen emerge from the bush. He still went to the car to get his gun. After all, he was in the middle of the streets in the dead of the night; he needed some form of security. He froze when he could not find the gun in the car. He suddenly remembered leaving the gun, as well as his bottle on the windowsill. "Oh, shit!" he swore angrily. He kicked hard against the car tyre. Could the night get any worse?

Pauline shrugged hard as she rubbed her tied hands against the dagger on the table. She had called for Vivian to help her after the intruder was gone, but it seemed that girl had her earpiece in her ears again and could not hear a thing. She knew she could not remain bound this way until morning, and hence she had to do something about setting herself free. Besides, there was so much going on, things that left her confused, and she needed to sort them out herself.

She hissed as she wounded herself against the dagger. She had lost count of how often this happened. Her wrist and hands were already bloodied as a result of this. She gave a sigh as the cloth finally came free of her wrist. She reached for her mouth and removed the cloth from it. She took a deep breath then stumbled out of her room.

She rushed to Vivian's room and opened it. Vivian got up from her bed and threw her an angry and disappointed look. "Pauline, this is indeed pure madness. I thought if you took your drugs all the time that your hallucinations would stop. What kind of rubbish have I gotten myself into?"

Pauline was silent. All she had wanted to tell her of her ordeal remained in her throat; she couldn't speak. She was in a terrible state, and all Vivian could think of was that she had gone crazy. Couldn't she see that something wrong had happened? As Vivian continued to rant, tears dropped down Pauline's cheeks and blood flowed from her nose. What was wrong with her, she wondered. Any sane person ought to know that this was not some joke. However, her injured and weakened sight did not move Vivian.

Vivian stopped as she noticed the drops of blood. She gave Pauline a look and walked past her. "How can you be so cruel? If you want to kill yourself, do you have to involve me? Don't you know I will be arrested? What kind of trouble do you want to put me in? What have I done wrong to you?"

She saw the drops of blood on the floor leading to Pauline's bedroom. She followed them to her room and opened the door. She was shocked as she stared at the room which was in disarray, as well as stained with blood.

"What have you done!?" Vivian yelled.

Pauline stared at her silently. Where would she even start from? If she told her all that happened, Vivian would still not believe her. She would only call her crazy, and tell her that it had all happened in her head.

"You don't want to talk!" Vivian chided. She stared at the dishevelled room. "See the work you have created for me? At times, you are like a demon. How can any sane person do such a thing to another human being? You just hate me. Yes, you just hate me. Or you're possessed by some evil spirit. Just know that I won't be cleaning this room alone. You will join me as well," Vivian continued. She threw her a glare and stormed out of the room, muttering.

Pauline locked the door behind her and went to the bed. She stared at the dagger, lost. Her arms throbbed with pain, but what was worse was the emotional battle she was going through. Her gaze suddenly dropped on the gun. She stared at it in surprise; the intruder must have forgotten it in his haste. She moved to it and took it. Her gaze also fell on the bottle, so she opened it and took a sniff. It didn't smell familiar and she had no idea what it was. She wondered what he had wanted to do with it. She kept it in a corner hoping it would be useful one day.

She moved back to the bed and stared at the gun. This was the first time she was able to see such a weapon at close proximity. She played with it in her hands as she contemplated what to do with it. Was it a blessing in

46

disguise, she wondered, a means to end all she was going through? She gently raised the gun to her head and closed her eyes. Her finger went to the trigger. A knock on the door startled her and pulled her out of her plans.

Vivian stood outside the room with a tray, on which there was a jug of juice and two glasses. Beside them was a bag of drugs. "Pauline, please help me open the door," Vivian called. When she got no answer, she balanced the tray on one side and attempted to open the door. It was locked. "Oh God, not again," Vivian groaned. "Pauline, open the door. Please don't start, I beg you."

Pauline remained in her position, oblivious to Vivian's pleadings to open the door. Looking at the door, she pulled the trigger. Her heart pounded as she heard the click.

Nothing happened. The chamber was empty of bullets. She lowered the gun and stared at it, dazed. She didn't know whether to be sad or relieved: sad that she had not killed herself with the opportunity she had or relieved that there was no bullet in the gun and that she had not stupidly ended her own life.

A memory occurred to her, taking her back to the past. She had been eleven and was in the living room watching a detective series. She watched every move the group of detectives made as they solved a murder. It was a British show which she loved because of the thoroughness of their work. The detective genre had become one of her favourites over the last few years and she spent hours, when not working on schoolwork, glued to the TV. As the group of detectives made their way to catch the killer in an underground railway station, she became agitated. She stood up and imitated them, stretching her fingers like a gun towards the TV.

She ran in front of a mirror to see if she was good at it like they were. "Freeze!!" she said in a British accent. "Your hands on your head!"

"Pauline!" her mother called from the doorway. Pauline turned around to see her mother with a smile on her face; she had no idea that she had been watching her.

Pauline ran to her mother laughing. "Mummy!"

"Well done, dear. You're becoming good at this. I want you to know that I am proud of you."

"Thank you, mummy," Pauline said, wrapping her arms around her mother's waist.

"I want you to always be strong and stand tall no matter the challenge that approaches you. You're a hero, my baby. You're the source of my happiness, my joy. The only thing in life that I am proud of."

"Thank you, mummy. I love you very much and I'm proud of you, too."

"I love you, too, baby. Mummy has a present for you. Go to my room and bring my red bag," her mother said.

Pauline quickly ran to the room and returned with a red bag. Her mother pulled a waterproof bag from it and gave it to her. Pauline hurriedly opened it and pulled out a detective movie and book. "Yeah! Mummy, thank you," she said, hugging her mother, who returned the hug, not wanting to let her go.

"Mummy, can I ask you a question?" Pauline murmured into her mother's hair.

"Sure, my daughter," Mrs. Griphix said pulling away from her.

Pauline bit her lips nervously. "Mummy, when will daddy stop beating you?" she broke into tears and her mother hugged her again.

"Pauline, I don't know. I truly don't know. But I pray to God that one day, women shall have equal rights in this country. I pray that one day women will be liberated from abusive marriages. I used to be an advocate for women's liberation until your father killed my dreams. I have no idea how I was blinded from my vision, but it happened. I pray to God that he gives you the strength to carry out my dreams. To right the wrong that I made."

Pauline shook her head. Oh, her poor mother, and to think she was now walking the same path her mother had once walked. It was history repeating itself again. She, however, knew that this was a wake-up call to her, that she needed to do something and change the story of her life, or she would be like her mother.

She reached for her phone which she had found by her room door. She had a few missed calls from her work colleagues. She ignored them and quickly went on the Internet. She searched anxiously for all she could find about Janet Cole. When she could find nothing in the tabloids, she went on Facebook and Twitter and stalked the accounts of those who knew her.

After a while of searching on the Internet, she found what she was looking for: some useful information. She was amazed by it, but understanding soon dawned on her. When she was done, she had a satisfied smile. She wrote down all she needed to know and what she had to do.

Then she got up and set about cleaning the room. In a few minutes, the room was in good shape. All that had been scattered by the man was put back into place. She went to the bathroom and attended to her injuries. She cleaned the blood off and placed bandages on them, then took an aspirin to ward off the pains. She also got a bucket of water and soap and mopped the room where it was stained with blood.

She left the room and went to the doorway and mopped it as well. She could hear Vivian in the kitchen moving about angrily. The younger woman stormed out of the kitchen and stopped when she saw Pauline cleaning the mess. She shook her head. "You just like giving other people problems, don't you? I am glad you're cleaning this mess. At least you have sense for once." She walked past her and closed the door to her room.

Pauline ignored her and continued what she was doing with a lot of thoughts running through her mind. She thought of how she had met Robert. It had been a bad time in her life when she was alone, as she had recently just lost her mother. He had come into her life and showed her love and attention, or at least she had thought that's what he was doing. They had met at a friend's birthday and he had gotten her number from her friend.

Truth be told, she had found him charming and handsome. She was a quiet, shy girl and had never had a man of his class and confidence approach her before. He had taken charge, knowing what was best for her, and she had followed everything he did. She had felt he knew her best and was in the right to decide for her. Even though she had felt something missing in their relationship, although she had felt a void, she had thought it was normal. After all, her parents' marriage had not been a bed of roses.

They had gotten married a few months later and it was then that Robert unleashed his true self. There were so many rules and regulations he had for her. As a matter of fact, he wanted her to change from the woman he had married to the woman he wanted to be married to. Her mental state of mind had never been an issue until a few months into their marriage when she could not take his abuse.

She had tried to voice it to those around them, but he had called her bluff and blamed it on the ordeal she had suffered as a child watching her father beat her mother, as well as her mother's death. The best thing, Robert had said, was to seek psychological help, and this she had done. He had been the one to choose the doctors and when he felt they were not helping; he began to get her drugs to handle her depression.

Her state only seemed to get worse with the abuse and neglect she received from him. He never failed to make it known to anyone they came across that something was wrong with her. He had once said that he was trying to protect her, and she had been so stupid that she believed him.

He had always been the one in charge for as long as she could remember, but not anymore. Things were about to change, and she was going to get her life back.

The intruder was still in the dark with his bonnet open. He had tried all he could to get the engine to start, but the car was still immobile. Even though it was cold outside, he was sweating as a result of working on the car. "Just my luck," he muttered. Everything had been going according to plan, but then the car stopped.

First, the engine had kicked, and then he discovered he had forgotten the gun in Robert's place. His hands slipped into his pocket and he brought out four bullets which ought to be in the chamber of the gun. When he had found out that Robert was not in the house, he had felt no need to use it. The last thing he had wanted was for it to go off and for someone to be hurt. Not that he cared, but the only person he was after was Robert. Robert alone was going to pay for what he had done. The damn gun had cost a lot, but he had no option but to get another one.

He looked around the dark road; only a few cars had gone by and none had bothered to slow down to offer him help. He perfectly understood their fear, as it was a quiet and dangerous area. He needed to get out of there before it got late and he would be vulnerable to men of the underworld.

He decided to make a last attempt at fixing the car. He tried to tweak the engine. It came alive and he rejoiced as he got in the car, but a second after getting in, the car died again. He cursed and hit the dashboard with fury. If he continued this way, he would spend the night on the corner of the road. He reached for his phone and called a number.

"Hello, I need your help..."

BEN DARKWA

CHAPTER 5

Pauline stepped out of her room with a smile. The smile transformed her face to that of a beautiful woman. She had on a lovely red gown which she had worn only once and had pushed to the back of her wardrobe, as well as a black pair of heels that she had not worn since she purchased them. Her makeup was perfectly done such that anyone who had seen her the previous day would not have known she was the same person. No longer were there bags underneath her eyes, as she'd had a perfectly healthy sleep. When she woke up, she had immersed herself in a warm bath after exfoliating her body.

Staring at herself in the mirror, she had realized that a lot of changes had needed to be made. But first, she would have to do what she had set her mind to. She locked her room door behind her and dropped the key in her bag. She went to the living room and put her bag down before going to the kitchen to get something to eat.

Vivian stepped out of her room and tiptoed to the living room. With her gaze on the kitchen door, she slipped her hand into Pauline's handbag and removed the room key. She hurried to the room and inserted the key. She heard Pauline got back to the living room and immediately left the door open to avoid any suspicion.

Munching a slice of bread, Pauline reached for her bag, dropped a bottle of water into it, and picked it up. "Vivian! Vivian!" Pauline called.

Vivian walked into the living room.

"Open the gate," Pauline said.

Vivian, however, stared at her, stunned. She looked very different, and if she didn't know her well enough, Vivian would have thought it was another woman. She was very beautiful. Vivian could not remember the last time she had seen her this way. As a matter of fact, she looked like she had not been crazy just last night. "Excuse me, ma'am. You... sound different, and you also look different. Is everything okay?"

Pauline gave her a stern look. "You heard me, didn't you? Go and open the gate!"

Vivian hurriedly walked out of the house to do as she had been instructed. Pauline followed her slowly, every step confident and fearless. The timid and crazy Pauline had gone away with the night. When she got outside, the gate was already opened. Pauline got into her car and sped out.

Vivian clapped her hands in wonder and placed them on her waist. "People that will see her now will not know she's mad." She shook her head, surprised. Pauline was acting so oddly. Vivian guessed it was the drugs that she was taking. She quickly closed the gate and hurried back into the house. She went to Pauline's bedroom door and opened it. She pulled her phone out of her back pocket and dialled a number. The receiver, however, refused to pick up. She rolled her eyes and set her eyes on a task.

She looked around and began to search the room. Every move she made was fast, as she knew she had no time. She suddenly froze when she heard a screeching sound of a car outside the gate. She shrugged then continued in her search.

She stopped when she saw a file in one of the drawers. She picked it up and flipped through it. She nodded in delight. This was what she was looking for. Vivian froze when she heard footsteps in the living room. From the sound of the heels, she knew Pauline was back.

Slowly and silently, she stepped out of the room and locked it behind her. She tiptoed to her room and dropped the file.

Pauline slipped her hand into her bag to get her key but could not find it. She looked confusedly at her bag; she knew she had kept the key in it before she left the house. She searched through the pockets of her bag but could not find the key. She removed everything from the bag, but yet could not find the key. Her eyes narrowed, confused. She knew she had to retrace her steps. She got up and went to the kitchen to check if she left it there.

Noticing that the place was clear, Vivian ran into the living room and placed the key in Pauline's bag then tiptoed out. Pauline walked back into the living room. She had not found the key in the kitchen. She went to the room door in the hopes that she had forgotten it in the mouth of the door, yet she did not see it. She twisted the handle but it refused to budge.

She went back to her bag and checked again for the key. She found it in one of the pockets. She sighed, relieved; today was not a day for mistakes, and she needed to keep her head in the game. She went to her room and opened the door. She picked up the book she had forgotten from the table; it was filled with all the information she had penned down last night.

She placed it in her bag and headed out of the house before driving off on a mission.

Vivian lay on the bed in her room, smiling. She had done it without being caught. "I am so clever," she said aloud. Her phone buzzed and she picked it up. It was a message from Thomas.

Thomas: You said you have news for me?

Vivian: Yes, I have found it. So, what's in it for me?

Thomas: Oh my God! Thank God! This is great. I'm coming over right now.

Vivian sat up straight immediately.

Vivian: You dare not enter this house. If my cousin sees you, he will kill you.

Thomas: Damn! So, how do I get it? Please, I beg you.

Vivian: Text me when you're close by. I will meet you outside.

Thomas: Okay, I am on my way.

Vivian: And you better not come here dressed like a clown. Put on your best outfit.

*

A very old-looking taxi was parked outside, opposite the gate. Inside, in the driver's seat, Thomas sat. His dreadlocks contrasted with the dark suit he was dressed in. The AC wasn't working and he was beginning to sweat. He tugged the tie on his neck down and shook his head. He picked up his phone and called Vivian.

"Hello?" she said.

"Vivi, I'm outside," he said.

"Better stay there, I will be there right away."

"Get ready for a surprise. I have a surpri…" He shook his head when she dropped the call.

When he heard the gate open, he adjusted himself on the seat and put on a serious look.

Vivian stepped out of the gate and looked around for Thomas. Where was he, she wondered. She reached for her phone and then stopped when she caught sight of him in the driver's seat of the taxi. Oh my God, she thought. She burst into laughter waving the brown envelope.

Thomas was so happy to see her that he could not stop grinning like a Cheshire cat. He stuck his head out of the window and called. "Hey baby, I'm here!!"

Vivian rolled her eyes. "Oh please, I'm not blind. I can perfectly see you in that junk of a car," she muttered. She locked the gate behind her and crossed the road to Thomas' car. She sighed as his eyes danced with excitement. She did not want to get into the car but it wasn't as if she had an option. She opened the passenger seat and got in.

"My baby! My Vivi," Thomas said, excited.

She, however, ignored him and folded her arms, staring straight ahead.

"What's wrong, baby? Why aren't you happy?" he asked.

"Do you want to explain why I am giving this to you? I hope you know the amount of trouble I will get into when he finds out it is missing," Vivian said.

He patted her fondly. "Don't worry, baby, I have a job now. All I need is this document your cousin took from me after we... fought," he said, gesturing at both of them.

Vivian glared at him. "Fought?! Are you even serious?"

Thomas averted his gaze.

"Good. Look aside in shame. You meant when you beat me up right? When you beat me up after I refused to tell you I was going to spend the night at my mother's place. Have you forgotten that I had to go to the hospital to treat my injuries? I am a Smith, remember? No one lays hands on a Smith without getting hurt. It just doesn't happen. At all. You're lucky the beating my cousins gave you was small; you better thank me for interceding for you. I know my cousin, and he would have done worse, he just decided to take your documents and not put you back in jail."

Thomas shuddered at the mention of jail. "All that's in the past, love. Why don't we forget about that, huh? I still love you no matter what, and I want you back. This time I promise to be on my best behaviour. I promise to do my best to avoid any dispute between us."

Vivian lifted a brow. "I will think about it. But don't expect me to give you an answer now. Anyway, here's your document." She waved the envelope at him. He reached forward to get the envelope and she moved it back.

"What do you want?" he asked.

"It will cost you a kiss and a surprise gift from you. By the way, what is this old thing?" she asked looking around the car with disgust. "This is a sorry excuse for a car."

"Of course I will have to give my baby girl a kiss," Thomas said excitedly.

Vivian laughed and handed the envelope to him. He took it and quickly opened the envelope. Inside were his passport, birth certificate, and some other personal documents of his. He smiled and screamed with excitement. "Oh my God! Thank you so much for saving my life, love." He stretched himself and turned his body towards Vivian for a hug. He hugged her tight and gave her a kiss. "Thank you, baby, thank you so much. You have saved my life. I have a surprise for you."

"Really?" Vivian asked excitedly.

Thomas nodded. "Yes, I have a surprise for you. Afterward, I will take you for a ride in this beauty. You may think it is a scrap but it is actually a beauty, baby. You will love it." He pulled out a sound system from under his car seat. He pressed the button and a song began to play. The loud music filled the air and he nodded to the tune of the song. He moved his head from side to side, shaking his body and shaking it well.

Vivian shook her head, amused. She loved his moves. He got out of the car and made a few moves like Michael Jackson, moving his body to one side and the other while attempting to moonwalk in the process. Vivian smiled. Then she regained her memory and shouted, "Get back in here, tiger!" The last thing she wanted was for some nosy neighbour to see them and tell her cousin, who would then figure everything out.

Thomas immediately stopped and got into the car. He huffed hard as he tried to regain his breath. "That...was for...you, darling..." he managed to stutter out. "Now, can I drive you around a bit?"

"Ok, if you insist. But not until I get my kiss," Vivian said with folded hands. He leaned forward to her and kissed her softly. "Please promise me you will not cheat on me again," she said in a soft and calm voice.

He nodded. "I promise you, babe, I really do love you," Thomas said.

Thomas drove the two of them around the neighbourhood. He sped around as fast as he could, trying to impress her. Vivian, however, held on tightly to the car seat for fear of her life. "Slow down, Thomas," she warned.

"No, baby, there's no need for that. We good, baby," Thomas said, smiling.

Vivian went pale and continued to clutch the arms of the chair. Suddenly, the car brakes failed. Thomas pressed hard on them to stop, but the car didn't stop. He pressed the brakes hard again, but the car once again refused to stop.

"What's happening?" Vivian yelled.

"I don't know!" Thomas yelled back.

Suddenly both of them screamed in fear. "Oh God! Blood of Jesus! Father God!" they yelled. Thomas tried harder to stop the car, but it was no use. As the car rolled down the road non-stop, a wet fluid spread through Thomas's trouser and he urinated on himself. A foul smell filled the car after he farted loudly.

"Jesus!" they both yelled, as the car ran into a wall, bringing it to a stop at last. Luckily, neither of them were hurt. Without wasting time, Vivian leapt out of her seat and grabbed Thomas by his dreads. She clenched her fist and smacked him hard a couple of times. Thomas screamed and she continued to hit him furiously.

"You fool! Idiot! Did they send you? So you're trying to kill me?" she cursed as she continued smacking him.

Thomas managed to extract himself from her hold. He panted hard. "I... am... sor... sor...sorry, baby."

"Sorry? You almost killed me in this junk heap you call a car! I should have known better than to get into this car with you!" Vivian shouted.

"I am sorry, baby," Thomas begged before he burst into tears ,which stunned Vivian. Snot began to pour from his nose. "Please baby, don't fight with me. I didn't mean for this to happen. All I wanted was to make you happy. Please, my legs could not reach far enough on the brakes. I don't even know what happened."

Vivian gave him a pitying look and reached for the door handle. Seeing him in such a state was pitiful; his urine already stunk in the car. She wondered what she had seen in him, but he was once a man she had loved. She shook her head as she got out of the car. Smoke had already started coming out of the engine. Thomas opened his car door and stepped out in a fit of coughing. He turned to look at the car, which was now smoking heavily. He placed his hands on his head in defeat. "Baby," he called to Vivian.

But Vivian was already walking away, back home. As he continued to call for her, she ignored him and walked on without looking back.

CHAPTER 6

Kizzie and Simon spared few glances at the TV. Their concentration was on the plates of food in front of them, covered in hot pancakes.

"I think you have to be careful," Kizzie said. She was a beautiful young woman in her twenties and was Simon's girlfriend.

Simon scoffed and Kizzie threw him a glare. "You're just too stubborn, you know. But you need to listen to me. You might end up in jail because of this."

Simon merely shrugged. Simon was tall and slim and had a crew cut. His eyes narrowed. "Kizzie, I don't care about going to jail. As a matter of fact, I am ready to drop my last blood to make sure that bastard pays for what he did. I will make sure I do anything I can to make Janet happy in her grave. I promised her that, and so I must."

"Come on, Simon," Kizzie admonished.

"Look, I will do it the easy way; the evidence I have been able to find should put him in jail. And if something happens that stops this from happening, then I have to do it my way," Simon said stubbornly.

"And what is your way? I am afraid to hear your response," Kizzie said.

Simon merely smiled coldly as thoughts ran through his mind.

"Come on, Simon. I hope you have no stupid thoughts in your head. You do realize you cannot fight evil with evil, right?" Kizzie chided her boyfriend.

"Who cares? The world has evolved. All I know is that that man must pay for his crimes, no matter what," Simon promised.

Kizzie could only take a deep sigh. She understood what her boyfriend was doing, but she wondered if he was going too far in the scheme. She knew, however, that she would only annoy Simon if she scolded him more. Once Simon set his mind to do something, he never failed.

*

Pauline looked at the address on the paper she held and nodded. She was at the right place. She was in Devtraco, one of the gated communities in the vicinity. She parked her car beside the gate then walked up to the gate of house number 21 and pressed the bell. It rang and she got no response. She rang it again and it took a while before the gate opened.

A young woman stepped out. She gave her a strange look. "Hello?" she asked.

"Hello!" Pauline said with a smile, putting on her new character. "Good day to you."

She nodded. "Yes, to you as well."

"Please, I am here to see Simon," Pauline said.

"Who are you, please?"

"Gina… Gina Lemon," Pauline quickly said with a smile while her heartbeat quickened.

The woman nodded. "Okay. Excuse me, I will be right back."

The gate closed and Kizzie went to the living room of the house. "Simon," she called.

"Yes, what's up babe?" Simon said, looking up from his laptop.

"There's a woman outside who's looking for you," Kizzie said.

"You don't know her?" Simon asked.

"No, haven't seen her before. I doubt she even knows you personally," Kizzie said.

"I doubt I know her then; I am not expecting anyone today. What's her name?"

"Gina Lemon," Kizzie answered.

"Gina Lemon?" Simon asked. He shook his head. "No, haven't heard the name before. Don't know who she is. Tell her I am very busy and cannot see her."

Kizzie returned to the gate. She smiled politely at Pauline. "Excuse me, I'm sorry, but he's really busy and cannot see you. Maybe you should come around another time," she added.

Pauline shook her head stubbornly. "He has to see me, it is very important that I meet with him. This is in connection with Janet."

Kizzie froze. "Janet?"

Pauline nodded.

"What about Janet?"

"That's why I have to see him," Pauline said.

"A second please," Kizzie said before shutting the gate in her face again. She jogged this time around to the house.

"Is she gone?" Simon asked as Kizzie came into the living room.

"Nah, she says she came here because of Janet," Kizzie said.

Simon froze. "Janet?" he asked.

"Yes, I am surprised as well. What do you make of this?" Kizzie asked.

"I don't know, dear, I really don't. You know, let me go and see who this woman is. I have no idea who she is but I am curious to see her and hear what she has to say."

Leaving Kizzie behind in the house, Simon went to the gate. He opened it to see a beautiful woman; she looked a little bit familiar, but he could not pinpoint where he had seen her before. If she was Janet's friend, he had probably seen her in a picture that Janet had shown him. "Hello?" he said. "I'm Simon Cole. Please come in. But I am very busy and have only ten minutes to spend with you. So, what is it you have to tell me?"

"I'm a friend of Janet's as well as a major business partner," Pauline lied. She held her breath when she was done. She hoped he had been unable to see through her lies. She let out a soft exhale of relief when Simon said, "Follow me."

She followed him into the compound and into the building to the living room. Kizzie nodded at both of them and Simon offered her a seat.

"Do you care for a drink?" he asked.

Pauline nodded. "Yes, a glass of juice will be okay if you have any."

Kizzie quickly got up and headed to the kitchen. She returned a minute later with a tray on which there was a container of cold juice, as well as a glass.

"Thank you," Pauline said. She opened the drink and poured some for herself, then took a sip.

"So?" Simon asked, getting straight to business.

"Well, I am Gina Lemon," Pauline said, making sure not to slip from her British accent. When she had learned how to talk like foreign actors as a child and took it on as a hobby, she had never known that it would come in so handy later on. For the first time, she was grateful for having picked it up. Pauline continued, "I have been in London for the past ten years."

"And how do you know Janet?" Simon asked.

"Oh, we have been friends since secondary school. Ashanti High," Pauline said with a confident smile. She had done enough research to make sure that they did not suspect that she was lying. "We have been in touch and have been talking about deliberating on business projects that the two of us would be working on when I arrived here. However, for some time now, she hasn't been answering my messages or calls. She has just been unreachable. I have been busy for a while, and since I just arrived here, I called an old friend who gave me your address. I hope you don't mind giving me her address so I can go see her."

Silence fell upon them. Pauline was stunned when she saw a tear drop fall down Simon's cheek. Kizzie who had been calm now looked sad. "Um... is something wrong? Why are you crying? What is happening, please?" she asked.

"Help bring my bag from my room," Simon said. Kizzie nodded and left them, returning a short while later. Pauline almost jumped from her seat when she saw her black bag with them. Everything came to her in an instant. It fit like a puzzle as she watched Simon search through her bag.

She could now remember why his voice had been familiar when she saw him. He was the intruder! Her body shivered in fear. She wondered if she was in danger. Couldn't he recognise her from last night? With the way he acted, she doubted it. The light had been dim and she had looked very haggard. Also with the remarkable makeup done, she knew she looked different. She, however, knew she could not take that chance, that she needed to be done and to be out of there as soon as she could be before he recognised her.

Simon handed her a newspaper page from the bag. It featured Janet Cole's obituary. Pauline's hand flew to her chest. "Oh my goodness! Janet, dead! Oh my God!" She shook her head in disbelief. "Tell me this is a joke! She was such an amazing woman."

Kizzie shook her head. "Sadly, it is the truth. Janet is no more."

"What happened to her? Was she sick or something?"

Simon shook his head furiously and spat out, "No she wasn't!" He pulled out of the bag a picture and handed it to her. Pauline was shocked once again, as she was staring at the face of her husband with his arms wrapped around Janet.

"Who's this?" Pauline asked nervously, as well as curiously.

"That's the man who killed her," Simon said with hatred. "That man beside her is a serpent, a bastard…"

"They look so happy," Pauline said, shaking her head. "How can that be possible? She told me she was seeing someone and was so excited about it. I never knew he was a monster. Please tell me he's behind bars."

"No, he isn't. That man's crafty. He murdered her and made it look like a suicide. But the Janet I know would never kill herself. Never! Especially with what was at stake. He killed her and the police say it is suicide. But don't worry, I have enough to send him behind bars." He picked out of the bag some pictures, two pen drives, CDs and a network chip. He handed the pictures to Pauline, who went through them. They were of Janet and Robert together in romantic poses. Pauline felt bile in her throat as she stared at them. She was disgusted at the sight of her husband with another woman.

"This is her phone," Simon said, waving a pink iPhone. "I recovered it from her room the day she died. It contains vital audio information. With this, justice shall be done for her."

"Do you mind if I listen to the audio?" Pauline asked.

"I am sorry, but no. At least not yet. When the time's right, everyone will know," Simon answered.

Pauline nodded in understanding. She stared at the pictures one final time before she passed them to him. "That man is a beast. He deserves to rot in prison. Poor Janet, she had no idea she was dating a monster."

Kizzie sighed. "And to think the bastard is a womanizer; he has a wife but keeps having affairs. Who knows how many women he has killed?"

Simon got up. "I was getting ready for a meeting when you dropped by and I need to leave for it soon. Perhaps we can meet another time?"

Pauline nodded.

"Please take down my number and keep in touch," Simon continued.

Pauline took out of her bag a pen and paper. She wrote down Simon's number as he said it to her. "Thank you for your hospitality. I am so sorry for your loss, but be reassured that he's going to pay. Now that I am in town, I will use all my resources to get to the root of this. By the way, I brought this from London; please keep it as a present. I will be staying around for a while but will make sure to call you up."

"Thank you," Simon said, taking the pen from her as well as Kizzie who she handed one to also. Simon turned to Kizzie and whispered something to her. In that moment, Pauline quickly pulled her phone from her bag and took a picture of Janet's phone.

"Thank you once again for coming. Please keep in touch for a drink before you leave for London. And please don't worry about getting involved in this, we're handling the matter and have everything under control. Soon he will be arrested," Simon added, with a smile which Pauline did not buy.

She said goodbye to Kizzie, and Simon led her to the gate and let her out. She got into her car and drove off. She realized she had been holding her breath when she let out a long sigh. "Oh my God!" she muttered, shaking her head. It had been like she had been in a den of lions. She had been so scared, but she had to go through with it. She was so glad that he had not recognised her. With his hatred for her husband, he could have done anything to her.

She parked the car in a corner and dialled a number. It rang once and she let out a smile when she heard Simon and Kizzie talking. The pens she had given them picked up their conversation and transmitted them to Pauline's phone for her monitoring. It was one of those little spywares she had gotten as a gift as a fan reward for one of her favourite detective shows. She had never thought she would use them until now. She smiled in delight, and then a little sorrow washed through her. This was a delicate matter and she had to be strong about it. With a deep sigh, she started the engine and drove off.

After a few minutes of listening to the pair's conversation, Pauline was sure that Simon had been the one who had broken into the house the previous night. Did she blame him? After knowing all that had happened, she didn't. Although she hated that he had scared her, she understood where he was coming from. She, however, had her own plans, plans she was going to follow through to the very end.

She ended the call, terminating her snooping on their conversation. She dialled a number and made another call. "Where are you?" she asked. She nodded as the receiver relayed to her his location. She continued driving until she stopped at a mall. She parked in the car park and made another call to the same receiver, then waited in the car.

In a minute, a young man in his early 20s with a hood on came into the park. He looked around as if wondering which car was hers. With two honks on her horn, Pauline signalled him to come over to her car. The young man moved to her car and she opened the passenger side for him to get in.

"Good day," Ben said.

She nodded in greeting and scribbled something on paper, then handed it to him. "And the picture of the phone?" he asked.

With Bluetooth in her phone, she sent the picture to him. "I need that phone urgently," Pauline said. "For now, he's under surveillance. I will keep monitoring him and will keep you posted on his movement." She pulled an envelope out of her bag and handed it to him. He looked into it and counted the money. He nodded at her and got out of the car.

Pauline watched him go. She really hoped she was doing it right, because for some things, there were no second trials. It was either you got it the first time or that was it.

PAULINE'S DIARY

CHAPTER 7

In a black car, Ben and Bilson sat 200 yards outside Simon's gate. The both of them smoked cigarettes, letting the smoke out the back windows. Although they pretended to mind their own business, attention was paid to the movement from Simon's house. They had been that way for hours since they had arrived that morning.

Ben's phone rang and he answered it. "Mam, good morning," he said.

"Good morning Ben. There has been a change of plans. Simon will be going out very soon, but he will be taking the phone and the other things with him. Hence there's no need to break into the house again."

"So, what do we do now?" Ben asked.

"Follow him and get the things from him. No use of violence, please. I want you to do it without anyone getting hurt. Understand?"

"Copy that," Ben said. It was even the best for him as he was not a fan of violence.

"Good, and please do not fail. If he finds out something is wrong, then he will make sure to secure it. Call me when you have it," Pauline said before hanging up.

Ben turned to his friend and told him about the change of plan. Between themselves, they discussed how they were going to get the phone from him. Chopping their knuckles with laughs, they decided on the perfect plan.

Just as Pauline had said, the gates of the house opened and a black car pulled out with Simon driving, with the window rolled down. Ben started the car and they followed him, keeping their distance without Simon noticinghe was being followed.

Simon reduced the volume of the music in the car when his phone began to ring. It was a strange number and it could be from one of his business clients. He parked the car so he could talk attentively to the caller. He did not see the other black car when it parked behind him.

Ben got down from the car and went over to Simon's. "Excuse me, sir," Ben said.

Simon looked up from his phone. The caller had ended the call immediately after he had answered. It probably was a wrong number. "Yes?"

"Please, I am a stranger in town. I am headed to Satellite Plaza, how do I get there please?" he asked. His gaze drifted around the car in search of the phone. It settled on the passenger's seat beside Simon. The pink phone rested there. Stretching his back, he signalled at Bilson who had been watching him closely.

"Oh, no problem. You're going in the wrong direction, however. You need to take a turn and take the other lane, then…"

As Simon continued to give directions to him, Bilson carefully and slowly let himself out of their car. He crawled below Simon's eye level to avoid being noticed. With Ben acting confused about the directions given to him and acting as a distraction to Simon, Bilson slowly rose up by the passenger door. With a swift move, he shoved his hand into the car window and took out the phone and began to run.

"Someone just took something!!!" Ben rose in an alarm. Simon immediately looked to the passenger seat, the phone was missing. Simon jumped out of the car and immediately chased after Bilson.

"Hey stop!!! Thief!!" Simon called after him. He pursued Bilson, running hard behind him, but the other man was a faster runner. The both of them fell to the ground and before Simon could deliver a blow to him, Bilson was already off on his way. He got into a bus which zoomed off. Panting, Simon sat on the ground trying to catch his breath.

Alone by the empty car, Ben looked around the car and spotted Pauline's black handbag which contained the remaining evidence. He grabbed the bag and rushed to his car and zoomed off. He called Bilson. "Where are you?"

"On my way to your place. I have the phone with me," Bilson said, breathing fast.

Tired and still breathing fast as well as being sweaty, Simon staggered back to his car. He was furious and his fist was clenched in anger. He stopped when he noticed that the stranger who had asked him for directions was gone. He immediately ran to the car. He cursed out loud when he noticed the black bag was gone. His wallet, his phone and his personal belonging were still intact, but all that had to do with his sister had been taken away.

"No!!!!" he let out in rage. He kicked the car angrily. Tears pooled in his eyes out of frustration. He had been so close, so close to sending that monster to prison. He wondered how he had fallen for their cheap trick. Now everything he had worked for was no more.

"Robert Smith," Simon said with hate. "I will hunt you down, I promise you. You might have outsmarted me today, but no more. I will see you in Hell," he promised.

*

After placing an order for breakfast to the receptionist, Robert pulled Selina to him and kissed her softly. He sighed when his phone rang interrupting them. He stretched his hand and took the phone from a bed. He rolled his eyes when he saw that it was one of his colleagues from work. Couldn't he call at a better time? As he answered the call, Selina's phone began to ring. She, however, spared the phone no glance, but went rather to the bathroom.

"I will call you later," Robert said, hanging up. He looked suspiciously at Selina's phone. Why had she not answered the call? He picked up the phone and went to her call logs. The call had been from an unknown number. Then he went to her messages.

Seeing nothing there, he went to her WhatsApp. The first message below his was from a man, Kofi Asante. He looked at their chat and calls history, it was a lot. His eyes narrowed with fury. He went through their messages and although there was nothing in them to suggest a romantic relationship between them, he was still angry. He did not like that another man was spending so much time with his woman. When he heard the door open, he quickly dropped her phone.

Selina walked to him and smiled. "Why do you have that frown on your face baby?"

"I hope you're not cheating on me with other men," Robert said.

Selina looked at him confused, then anger took over as her eyes turned red. "What kind of stupid question is that? Are you for real? How can you..." She cried when

Robert's hand struck hard against her cheek. She held her cheek and looked at him scared. Tears pooled in her eyes.

Realizing what he had done, Robert begged, "I am so sorry, honey. I shouldn't have done that to you." He reached for her, but Selina moved away on the bed glaring at him.

"You slapped me," Selina muttered.

He reached for her and hugged her before she could pull away. "I am sorry honey. Seriously. You know I love you so much and I will be marrying you soon. Once my divorce goes through with Pauline, I am all yours. I am sorry for laying my hand on you, but I am just so frustrated that I am married to that psycho that I took it out on you. It won't happen again, I promise."

Selina nodded. "I accept your apology but please don't hit me again, that's something I cannot tolerate."

Robert kissed her. "Never, baby, I wish I could take that slap back. I would never hit a woman. Never. I love you, baby," he continued.

Selina smiled at him, then frowned.

"What is it?" he asked.

"Your wife; when are you going to divorce her? I am tired of waiting, you know. I want you all to myself. I don't want to share you with that crazy woman. I want you with me all the time, baby," Selina whined.

Robert patted her. "My love, very soon. All you have to do is to be patient. You know she's crazy, so I need to do this carefully."

Selina nodded. "I will be patient.

*

Pauline parked in front of the police station. She took a deep breath and closed her eyes. This was it; she had come this far and wasn't going back. She grabbed her bag and stepped out of the car, then climbed the stairs into the station.

"Good afternoon, officer," she said to the duty officer at the front counter.

The older man nodded at her. "Good afternoon madam. How can I help you?"

"I'm here to report my husband for domestic violence against me and also to reveal him as the murderer of a woman, Janet Cole."

The officer looked up in surprise. "What did you say?"

"I said I am here to file a charge of domestic violence against my husband and to reveal him as the murderer of a woman, Janet Cole," Pauline said repeating herself.

"I will be back, let me get the person in charge. Please wait," the man said before leaving. He returned a few minutes later with a tall and older man.

"I am Officer John," he said introducing himself. "Let's speak somewhere private."

Pauline followed him to an interview room. It was well lit and had just one window. They sat opposite each other around a table. "Go ahead, make yourself comfortable. I understand you are here to report a crime?" Officer John asked.

Pauline nodded. "Yes, I am." She pulled her laptop and the items she had gotten from Ben and his friend

Bilson out of her bag. They were more than enough to send her husband to jail. She put on the laptop and positioned the screen for both of them to see. "The reports are about the same person, my husband. I was a victim of domestic violence at his hand…"

"You have come to the right place madam," the officer said. "It is my job to help women like you. Can you tell me what's going on?"

"My husband has been abusing me physically, mentally, emotionally, sexually and any way you can name it," Pauline said.

"First of all, what is your name?" the officer asked opening a notepad with a pen ready to write down her personal details.

"Pauline, Pauline Smith," Pauline answered.

"Age?"

"29."

"Name of your husband?"

"Robert Smith."

He went on to ask for her house address which she provided and he wrote down. "Do you live together?"

"Yes, we do but my husband is on a trip at the moment."

"Tell me about the latest abuse you received from him. I need to know where it took place, what he did and if you have any evidence as to it."

Pauline froze. Her body shuddered as she recalled the event. It was something she wanted to put behind her, in her past. But if she needed the officer to take her serious, she had to tell him what had happened.

"Take your time madam," Officer John said.

Pauline nodded. "It took place in our home. In our bedroom... He... he... he raped me," Pauline said pushing back her tears. "I struggled against him and tried to scream but he covered my mouth and hit me when I fought against him. I was badly hurt not only physically but also psychologically."

The officer handed her a tissue roll. "I am sorry about your ordeal."

"Thank you," Pauline said. She took from the tissue and cleaned her eyes. She reminded herself that she needed to be strong. Her weakness was Robert's strength.

"And when did this happen?" he asked.

"Two weeks ago," Pauline answered.

"Sexual abuse is very serious. Did you report it to anyone? The police? Your doctor? A friend?"

Pauline shook her head. "No officer. I was scared. I was afraid that he would kill me. I believe my fears were rightfully founded after I found out he was the one who killed Janet Cole. I have evidence of it right here."

"We will come to the murder part in a while madam. So you don't have any evidence of any of your abuse cases at all? Not even a visible bruise?"

"He was always careful to hurt me in places no one would see, and if it did manage to show, he blamed it on me," Pauline said. She neglected to add that as a result of her mental state of mind, people tended to believe him.

"Okay mam, so this murder you're talking about. Where's your evidence?"

"Right here," Pauline said. She inserted a pen drive into her laptop but nothing showed on the screen, it was empty. She tried the other one and it was blank. She pressed the power button on Janet's phone but it refused to come up. She pressed it harder but it still remained blank. Her heart pounded fast; this could not be happening to her at such a time.

"What's happening madam?" the officer asked.

Pauline shivered. "I don't know; it is supposed to be here. I don't know…"

The officer looked at her strangely. "Mrs. Smith, are you on any medication at the moment?"

"Yes, I'm," Pauline said.

"Oh, for what if I must ask," he continued.

Pauline could see where he was going to, she, however, answered, "For depression. You see being with Rob has caused me a lot of turmoil that I have to seek medical help."

"I'm so sorry to hear this. But I believe you're not in a right state of mind…"

"No officer, I am mentally firm right now. I know what I am saying. My husband is a murderer, I just need some time to sort this all and I will give you evidence," Pauline objected.

The officer sighed. "I have other things to handle madam and right now all you have are accusations. They won't hold in any court." He removed a card from his pocket and handed it to her. "This is my card. You can contact me the next time your husband abuses you."

Pauline could see the pity in his eyes. He probably thought she was crazy, just like many thought. Under his gaze, she packed her things into her bag and left the station. It took her a lot of strength not to breakdown. I am not going to be defeated, she told herself repeatedly. Those who she had thought would protect her had not done so. It was now up to her to make sure everyone knew who her husband really was. She wasn't going to give up now. Never!! She told herself. She was going to find other ways to make sure justice was served. All it required was some time and careful planning.

She headed to the beach and sat by the shore trying to get herself together. She was indeed disappointed with the police, but she wasn't going to quit.

"I am going to survive," Pauline told herself. She had gone through a lot under her husband and still yet had survived. She recalled what her mother had told her, she had to fight out. She was not going to end up like her mother.

Thinking of her brought tears to her eyes. Although her father had died when she was fourteen, the effect of her father's abuse had continued for years later. Her mother had never been the same again. The effect of his abuse turned her into a wretched woman, her only solace had been her daughter and that had not even been enough.

She had only been thirty-five but she looked a decade older. She had been unable to trust any man because of her past experience. Nor had she been able to open up to others as her husband had succeeded in alienating her from others. It had been an ordeal and Pauline had watched the life in her mother's eyes fade.

When she had turned seventeen, her mother died. Pauline returned one afternoon from school very early to find the police around. They had tried to stop her but she had fought her way through. Her mother could not take it anymore and had killed herself. Pauline knew it had been from a broken heart. She had suffered till the very end.

"I will survive," Pauline said again, this time with more confidence. She took a stroll around the beach and rested for a while. When she got up from the sand, ready to go home, it was already night. She increased the music volume when she got to the car and sang in a high pitch voice, not caring if her voice was horrible as she drove. All that mattered was her will to break loose from the shackles of her life.

Her car almost came to screech, slamming against another car when she spotted something from her rear view mirror.

"Are you crazy?" a driver yelled.

"Sorry!" she yelled back as she reversed the car. She slowed down when she spotted a blue car in the parking lot of a bar. Wasn't that Robert's car? She wondered. She got down and moved closer to the car. She read the driver's plate and nodded; it was his. She looked carefully at the car in case she was mistaken. But she wasn't. It was her husband's car. Didn't he leave? She scoffed, of course, he had deceived her. Why should she have expected more from him?

She got into her car and parked at a building beside the bar where her car could not be spotted. She pulled out her makeup set and refreshed her looks. Thankfully, she had some clothes in the back of the car which she had just newly purchased and she slipped into them. To finalize her looks, she added a pair of contact lens which totally transformed her. Pauline gave herself a thumb up sign when she saw herself in the mirror. She couldn't even recognize herself.

She walked back to the bar on stilettos and got into the building. The smell of smoke first greeted her and she coughed as she tried to adjust to it. Loud music filled the bar from the speakers stationed around the room. It was very busy and almost filled up and she felt out of place. She, however, looked around trying to spot her husband who was supposedly on a trip.

Her eyes narrowed and her heart clutched when she spotted him. He had his arms around a woman who he was laughing and talking with. A spasm of jealousy waved through her, he had never been this way with her, even when he had been courting her. But then, with the discovery of the past days, she doubted she knew the man who was her husband. Robert signalled to the barman, who produced another round of drinks while Robert kissed the woman with him. She quickly pulled out her phone and took several shots of them.

Her heart leapt when she felt his gaze on her. Did he know she was the one, she wondered. Had he seen her? She quickly turned around and headed to the bar. She sat at the counter and ordered a light drink. Her fingers throbbed on the table as she wondered what she was going to do now.

"Baby I need to go to the bathroom," Selina said.

"Sure, I will be waiting," Robert said. Immediately after she left, he got up and approached the bar.

BEN DARKWA

CHAPTER 8

"Hi," a voice said behind Pauline startling her. She knew that voice perfectly well; it was her husband's. Did he know who she was?

"Hello?" he called again behind her.

Slowly, and while praying, Pauline turned around. "Hello," she said in her British accent.

A wide smile spread on his lips. "I saw you when you walked in. You're incredibly beautiful you know; anyone ever tell you that?"

Pauline let out a breath of relief. He did not know who she was. She was, however, angry that he was trying to flirt with her. He was not only married, but he also had another woman with him in the bar and was flirting with yet another. How shameless he was!!

"Thank you," Pauline said with a smile she did not mean.

"I am Rob, and you are?" Robert asked.

"Gina, Gina Lemon," Pauline said.

"Such a nice name for a beautiful woman like you, I have to say. I know I said it before, but you're really beautiful, you know. Can we... err... be friends?" he asked.

"No problem, I am cool with that. Are you alone?"

"Sure, I am. But I met an old classmate of mine here, and we're just cracking some bottles, you know what I mean," he added with a laugh.

Pauline laughed. A classmate he had been kissing. How naïve did he think she was?

"Please tell me you're alone," Robert said pleadingly.

"Yes, I just decided to come here and treat myself. You know, once in a while, you need to take care of yourself."

"Well, you can join our table if you don't mind. I would like to spend some quality time with you." He was interrupted by his ringing phone. "Excuse me," he said, bringing his phone out of his pocket. Robert's eyes narrowed as he stared at the caller. He looked up and saw Selina waving at him to come back to their table. "Seems my friend is back; do you mind joining our table?" he asked.

"No, but I can't stay for long," Pauline said.

A glimpse of joy appeared in his eyes that made Pauline feel disgusted. She picked up her drink and bag and followed Robert to his table. She could see the annoyed look Selina threw at her; if eyes were bullets, Pauline was sure to die a thousand times.

"Selina, meet Gina Lemon," Robert introduced.

Notwithstanding her dislike for Pauline, Selina reluctantly shook her hands.

"Nice to meet you," Pauline said. Of course, it was nice to meet with her husband's mistress.

"So Gina, where are you based? You don't seem to be from around here with your accent," Robert pointed out.

"I'm based in the UK. London, to be precise," Pauline said.

"That's so nice. You know, I have a project I am undertaking in London. I will discuss it with you as we build a trustworthy relationship," he said with a wink, which did not escape Selena, who scoffed.

"I love the word trustworthy, do you know why?" Pauline asked.

Robert shook his head. "No."

"Trust is the most powerful tool used as mortar for the foundation of every relationship. Once broken, it begins to wither. It is hard for it to ever be the same again."

Robert laughed nervously. "You're very intelligent; that was very philosophical.

Pauline nodded. "Anyway, we will see how it goes," she added a wink, which made Selina glare at her. Although she was angry, she was deeply amused. Here she was sitting down chatting with her husband and his mistress. While her husband flirted with her, his mistress despised her. How ironic.

They talked for a while, with Pauline being the centre of the discussion. She could see that the other woman truly despised her, and she couldn't help but laugh silently. As much as she wanted to play around with them, she knew she needed to go before she slipped and did something that could reveal her true identity. "I have to start going and head back to my hotel; I have a busy day ahead of me tomorrow and I need to be prepared."

"Oh, that's sad. When do we meet again?" Robert asked.

"We will surely meet; I will give you a call. Why don't we take selfies? I had so much fun today," Pauline suggested.

Robert literally jumped out of his seat. Ignoring Selina, he stood by Pauline who took a few shots of them with her phone. She took his number and waved at the both of them before she headed out of the bar. She got into her car and let out a burst of laughter. "Robert," she said shaking her head. She truly had no idea who the man she was married to was.

Back in the bar, Selina was furious with Robert. She grabbed her bag from the table and walked off to the car. Robert sighed, why was she acting like a baby he wondered. He paid the bills and headed outside to join her. He had to admit, Gina was quite attractive. He would like to have something to do with her, and he had a feeling she would be able to help with his business in the UK. He regretted not taking her number but giving her his. He could only hope that she gave him a call.

"I can't believe you were flirting with another woman!" Selina yelled when he got to the car.

"I was not flirting with her, can't you see that what we have is a business relationship?" he asked. He was not in the mood for Selina's jealousy.

"I know what I saw; you were practically undressing her with your eyes. I can't believe you're such a coward..." She yelped when a hard slap cut across her cheek. She looked stunned at him and her eyes began to swell with tears. "You... slapped me..."

Robert sighed; he reached for her and hugged her. "Come on, baby; you know you have nothing to be jealous of. You were just reading into something that doesn't exist. I love you and my eyes are for you alone. The only thing I saw in that woman was a business connection; she could make my business expand. Don't you want us to be successful?"

Selina nodded.

"Good, you have no reason to be jealous. She's not even my type. All I care about is you, babe, and you alone," Robert said.

"You promised never to hit me," Selina said.

"And I'm sorry, it was a mistake. I have no reason for hitting my baby, you know I love you." He kissed her and she smiled. He, however, could not understand why she was always stubborn and not submissive. He liked her, no doubt a lot, among all the women he had been with. But she needed to accept her place. He knew in no time she would understand and accept who he truly was, just as Pauline did.

Thinking of her made him grimace. For the past few days he had completely forgotten about her and had not called home. He doubted anything had happened, after all, Vivian had not called him. This time around she had been good. He, however, knew it was time for him to head back home.

*

Pauline giggled at the scene on the TV. She shook her head amused. Her gaze drifted to the centre table on which was a brown A4 sheet sized sealed envelope with no address on it. A wide smile spread on her face when she heard a car horn at the gate; her darling husband was home.

Vivian walked out of her room and went outside to open the gate. The blue car drove into the compound. "Welcome," Vivian greeted, biting her lips hard. She had not expected him home so soon, what was she now going to do when he found out those documents were missing? She had thought about it and had decided that she would blame it on Pauline. Yes, that was what she would do. Even if her uncle did not truly believe it, at least his wrath would be on his wife.

"Thank you, how has my wife been?" Robert asked.

"Just there," Vivian said. She was not going to tell him that Pauline was doing perfectly well because it would destroy the lie she was cooking up. The woman's transformation had stunned her. It was like she was someone else entirely, and it worried Vivian. She had asked her what had happened, but Pauline had barely given her a blank look and then returned to what she was doing.

"Okay, bring my things from the car and take them to my room," Robert said, walking to the house. "Hello, darling," Robert said when he got in, with a sweet voice and a smile. He, however, got no reply as Pauline ignored him. "Baby, I have really missed you. How is your health?" he asked. He was met with silence again. "Aren't you happy to see me?" he asked.

Receiving no response, he walked to the couch she was seated in and sat beside her. Her gaze was on the TV like he did not exist. Vivian walked into the house and kept his things in the room then returned to the living room. "Cousin Rob, mummy is still not well and I have been unable to see her since. Now that you're home, I'm off to see her. I will be spending the night there and will be back first thing in the morning."

Robert nodded. "My regards to her, tell her I just got back from a trip and will get around to seeing her during the week."

Vivian nodded and headed out of the house. At least she was going to be away from his wrath if he discovered the documents were missing tonight, she thought as she hurried away. Robert turned his attention to his wife. "Baby, what's wrong with you? You haven't responded to me," he said.

Breaking her silence, Pauline said, "You really sound more romantic than ever, Rob. What has changed?" She sniffed the air. "Or are you drunk?"

"How can you ask me such a silly question?" Robert yelled. He waited for Pauline to apologize or to lower her gaze from his, but he was shocked when she did neither. In his anger, he raised his hand to hit her. He was shocked speechless when she grabbed his hand with her left hand, halting his attempted assault. He stared at her, shocked; this was not the wife he knew. Never had she stopped any assault of his.

"Never, and I repeat it, never in your life will you ever hit me again, or any other woman," Pauline said, then slowly released his hand from her grip. Turning back her attention to the TV, she added nonchalantly, "Anyway, you're welcome back from your trip."

Robert, however, continued to stare at her, surprised. He looked at the hand she had held and then back to her. This was not the wife he knew; she looked and seemed different. He wondered what had happened in the few days he had left to be with Selina. It wasn't something he liked. She had not threatened him directly, but he had felt the impact of her words. He was going to watch her closely and see what she was up to with her newfound confidence which irritated him.

The credits of the movie began to roll and Pauline reached for the envelope on the centre table. She handed it to Robert who looked at it, confused and curious. "What is this?" he asked.

"A young girl came to the house, and she said she had some important documents for you," Pauline said with a shrug.

Probably something from work, he thought, but they knew better than to send official documents to his home instead of the office. He looked at it for any address but could find nothing; it was plain. He opened it and saw some pictures. He removed them from the envelope and stared at them with shock.

One was the picture of him and Gina Lemon at the bar. A few others were of him and Selina kissing in the bar, while others were of the both of them kissing outside the bar. The last ones were of both of them going into the hotel. The date and time of the pictures were displayed at the bottom of the pictures. He was shocked; what did this mean, he wondered.

"Any problem?" Pauline asked.

He shook his head.

"Can I have a look at them?" Pauline asked.

"No!" Robert almost screamed, clutching the pictures to his chest.

Pauline pulled some pictures from under the centre table and arranged them on the table, they were the same as the ones Robert had in his hands. "Is this what you're trying to hide from me? Don't bother, I have seen them all."

Robert swallowed. He was confused about what was going on. "Pauline, what's going on here?" he asked.

Pauline laughed without mirth. "I'm only displaying selfies at the marketplace. Isn't it amazing?"

He got up and walked towards the hallway to their bedroom. Pauline called after him, "Do you want to tell me about how Janet Cole died?"

Robert froze in shock, then hurried to the room.

CHAPTER 9

A gasp escaped Robert when he got into the room. Everything was scattered and a dagger was stabbed on a table. "What the heck?" he cursed. His eyes went to his wooden box and he cursed again when he found it open. What had happened in his absence?

Pauline stopped outside the room door. She heard his curse and smiled, as he had found his welcome gift. She had taken so much delight in scattering things around the room, just as Simon had done that night. She wondered what was going through his mind. He probably thought this was something he could overcome. Not this time around.

As she entered the room, she dialled Officer John's number. She had called him earlier in the day and told him she would be calling later on.

"Officer, please stay on the line when I call. You may think I am crazy, but I am not," she had begged.

He had sighed but had agreed. "I will, but please do not waste my time," he warned.

She hid the phone under a blanket where she knew Robert would not notice and the officer could hear perfectly well. She sat close to it, relaxed, watching her husband's confusion.

"What happened here?" Robert asked. "Was there a break-in? Why didn't you or Vivian call me?" he asked.

Pauline ignored his questions. Rather she removed the iPhone which belonged to Janet Cole from her pocket. Janet had made a terrible mistake that day; she had no idea until she went home after being at the station that the phone was dead. It had taken her a few hours of charging before she could access the phone. She pressed the play button on the recording and the conversation filled the room.

Robert became still in surprise. The words were familiar to him, and they reminded him of that day. He had gone over to Janet's place after she had called him several times and sent him several texts that she was going to confront Pauline if he refused to make an honest woman out of her.

"Look, Janet, you have to be mature about this. You have always known that I am a married man. There's no two ways about this, you need to get rid of this baby, and the earlier you do it, the better for the both of us, you especially," Robert said.

"No way, Robert! There's no way I am going to abort my three-month-old baby. You just have to be kidding about this. How cruel can you be? This is your child! Your son or daughter, and you want me to kill it! I am so disappointed in you, Robert!" Janet yelled at him.

Janet let out a cry when he slapped her, pushing her to the bed. She clutched her face as tears ran down her cheeks. "You slapped me," she cried, staring at him with anger and disappointment.

Robert got on the bed and hugged her. "I'm so sorry, baby, I didn't mean to do it. You just annoyed me. Forgive me, love. But you need to understand that this is for the best of both of us."

Janet pushed him away and glared at him. "Don't you dare touch me! I hate you! I can't believe I fell for your stupid tricks. You continued to deceive me, you promised me you would leave your wife, but you have only been leading me on all this whole time. Simon, my brother, will hear of this. And I assure you, you're going to be in very deep trouble!"

Robert sighed. "Come on, love; it hasn't gotten to that extent yet. You know I'm sorry that I reacted this way.

It wasn't meant to be. Like I said, I was angry. Today has been a stressful day. Forgive your darling, Janet."

Janet averted her gaze from him and stared at the wall, still fuming.

"Seriously, I am sorry, love. I admit it, I have been stupid. This child is going to be a blessing for us. I accept the pregnancy. You're going to be the mother of my children. Come on, come to me baby," Robert said with a smile.

"You sure? You are not joking with me?" Janet asked.

"Of course not! We're going to be a happy family," Robert said as she got into his embrace. "You know I love you."

"I love you so much," Janet said, resting her head on his shoulder.

"Now you need to rest. A baby is not an easy thing to care for, you know. Let me get some water for you to drink, love," Robert said. He walked away to the kitchen and opened the fridge. He opened a bottle of water and poured it into a glass. Staring at the door, he pulled out a little sachet and poured it into the water then swirled it around with a spoon.

"Come on, drink some water to calm your nerves," Robert said, handing her the glass when he returned to the room. She took a sip from it and he smiled. "Drink everything, I have heard water is good for babies. They grow up strong and healthy."

Janet smiled at him then gulped the rest of the water down. "Thanks," she said, handing him the glass which he kept on a table. "So what are we going to name our baby? I want Jackie if it's a girl and Noah if it's a boy. What about you?"

Robert smiled and humoured her as they talked about their unborn child. Suddenly, she let out a gasp. Then another. Her hand stretched forward for help as she continued to gasp. "Robert, please call the doctor, I can't breathe…"

Robert laughed and pushed her away. "Bitch! You really think I was going to marry you, huh? You're so foolish! Look at you now, gasping for breath, whereas before you were whining and threatening me a while ago.

You will die, Janet. The poison I gave you will kill you in a few seconds," he added with a laugh.

Janet stared at him, shocked. She could not believe that the man she loved was killing her. "Please," she begged. "I don't want to die. Our baby…"

Robert, however, ignored her. He didn't care a bit about her or their unborn child. She continued to gasp and it got worse as her internal organs began to fail. In her attempt to get help, she fell off the bed and began to crawl to the door. But it was too late, the poison had already taken over her system. "Rob," she let out one final time before death found her.

Robert walked to her and checked her pulse. She was dead. "Finally, she's dead," he muttered. He moved her to the bed and dropped her there. Then he placed the poison by the glass. He took from his pocket a suicide note he had penned down. He had not meant to kill her, but he had come well prepared in case she refused to listen to his reasoning. It was too bad that she had been stubborn, if not it may have worked between them. Now it was onto the next lover.

He went to her wardrobe and searched around for anything that could betray his presence. When he was done he packed them into a bag. With a final look, he stepped out the door. What he, however, failed to miss was her phone recording under her bed. Janet had been meaning to make good on her threat. In the event that he refused to marry her, she was going to send her conversation to his wife. But her plan was thwarted by the cold hands of death.

*

Pauline ended the audio and the room was filled with silence. Robert aged a decade with what he had heard. He had no idea that Janet had recorded their last conversation. He had confessed to the killing on a recording which was now in his wife's possession.

He had no idea how she had come across the recording, but he knew he had to make sure that she did not get it to the authorities. He fell to his knees and broke into tears. "Pauline, love, I am so sorry. I know I have been an asshole with the way I have been treating you. Please forgive me. It was a mistake, Pauline. Believe me…"

Pauline scoffed.

"I am truthful, love. It wasn't my intention to kill Janet. All I wanted was to get rid of the pregnancy. That's all. Please, ignore what you heard. I wasn't in my right frame of mind. Believe me. Don't let this get outside. This will damage my integrity, my personality, my career, my company and our marriage. Everything I have ever worked for. You know I am about delving into politics. Please love, you have to give it to me, we need to destroy this and put it behind us."

Pauline laughed. How stupid he thought her to be. He had carried out premeditated murder and was claiming all he wanted to do was get rid of the baby. He had killed his own flesh and blood. Even though she had not liked Janet, after listening to the recording, she had cried, she had wept for a woman who had not deserved death and even more for a child who had suffered death at the hands of his or her father.

How heartless her husband was. He was a monster! She looked at his tear-stained face, and she knew he did not feel remorse for what he had done. All he cared about was his reputation, nothing more. He didn't care for all the evil deeds he had done. She wasn't fooled by his sad look, for so long she had been a victim of his manipulation, but no more.

"Who's Selina? Or better still, Gina Lemon? The women you were frolicking about on your supposed trip out of town when you were having fun?" Pauline asked.

Robert's face lowered in shame, he averted his eyes from her not wanting to look her in the face.

Pauline shook her head with pity, hatred and disappointment at him. For so long she had loved him and had accepted his flaws as her fault. Instead, they had all been on him. For a while, she had worried herself on why she had been unable to bear him a child. Now she realized that it was only God's blessing.

No doubt she would love any child of hers, but Robert did not deserve to be a father. He was an egoistic man who cared for no one but himself. "Trust..." Pauline started. "Is the most powerful tool used as mortar for the foundation of every relationship. When it is broken, it begins to wither and can never be the same again."

Robert's eyes narrowed at her words. He had heard those words before, from Gina. He had no idea what was going on; there was so much he did not know. Like how his wife had come into the recording and what she wanted to do with it. She could not be stupid! He was all she had, so there was no way she could tell him. But it wasn't his fault that he had turned out the way he did. He looked up with sincere tears this time around.

"I grew up to see my dad beat my mother all the time. He trained me that a man should always be in control. Only this way can he have total respect. I was trained in a home where the woman did not have a say. A home where she was to follow everything said without objecting regardless of if I was leading her astray. A man's word is to be key to her. A man alone has the final say and knows best.

And once, I slipped. I went against my father's advice and fell in love with a woman. I went through years of pains for her while she took advantage of me. What did I not do for her? I even invested my tuition fee my father gave for a business of hers. And what did she do? She told me to my face that I did not deserve her. She made a mockery of me and cast me aside. I decided then that I was not going to be taken for a ride, I was going to always be in control."

Pauline felt pity for her husband. This was a side of his life she had never heard. She, however, knew that his past experience did not justify his actions. No one deserved to suffer in his hands because he had gone through a nasty experience. "You may have gone through a bad past, but there's always an end to nonsense. You met me, a woman who loved you dearly, but you didn't care about me. You have continued to hurt unsuspecting victims, all in your quest for supremacy. The law might seem silent, but it is not dead. It is time for you to face up to your crimes Robert," Pauline said.

Robert staggered up from his position. He wiped away the tears on his face. He had done his best to get his wife see reason, but she continued to be stubborn. "Pauline, please give me the phone. Give it to me and all will be well. All of this will go away. Don't let me do what I don't want to do."

Pauline chuckled. "What are you going to do, Rob, that you haven't already done? Kill me, too? The same way you killed Janet? You never change, do you? And they say I am the crazy one. The shrinks will have a field day with you!"

Robert glared at her, then he laughed wildly. "What do you think is going to happen? That I will let you hang me? Of course not! You're nothing! You know I never loved you. I just wanted a woman I could control and you fit perfectly. Oh, it was so much fun to break you from the strong woman you claimed to be. You're very silly, I must confess. You should be happy that I stuck around with you for this long. No!" he said, laughing. "I'm not going to kill you. You're going to kill yourself. You're such a fool! Who doesn't know you? Who doesn't know that you're a crazy woman, huh? All I was doing was defending myself, nothing else. You have a track record of mental illness, thank goodness, so this is all easy for me!"

Pauline shivered at his words. Sure, she knew what her husband was capable of, but this was first-hand experience with him and it scared and shocked her.

"You have one choice, Pauline, just one choice, woman. You either hand me that recording, and all will be well. We will act like this didn't happen, and we will be back to being the perfect couple we were. Who knows, I might not hit you as often as I used to. And if you're too stupid to take this opportunity, know that you will see hell tonight. I will kill you and I will have so much joy ridding the world of you. And in your place will be Selina. A better woman and a better wife while you're in heaven knows where," Robert spat out. "So, what's your choice woman?"

"Go to Hell!" Pauline shouted at him.

He moved towards her and she could see the fury in his eyes. She knew without a doubt that he would kill her and would feel no remorse, it was up to her to protect herself. She quickly picked up the bottle Simon had left behind the day he broke into the house. She wondered why the police had not arrived. A sinking feeling overtook her as she realized she may be on her own, the officer must have hung up a long time ago. She was, however, not going to go down without a fight!

She looked curiously at Robert when he went to the wardrobe. She swallowed when she saw him put on gloves. Before she could leap for the door, he sprung upon her. He grabbed her neck and began to strangle her.

Pauline coughed and struggled against him choking as his grip on her tightened. She fought hard against him and he flung her against a wall. A piercing pain flashed through her as she gasped for air. Robert reached for the phone and she managed to pick herself up from the ground.

She hit the bottle hard against his hand breaking it in the process with the unknown substance pouring on his hand.

"Argh!" Robert screamed in agony immediately after the substance touched his hand. The glove was of no help to him. He quickly removed it from his hand and flung it to the ground. He continued to scream at the excruciating pain as his hand burned. It turned black and was filled with wounds.

Taking the opportunity of his weakness, Pauline kicked him hard in the groin. He let out a gasp as he fell to the ground clutching his manhood with his other hand, while he waved the other injured and burning hand.

"Witch! Witch! I will kill you!" Robert yelled. He staggered up and rushed to the side of his bed. He pulled a gun from under a panel and cocked it. He swung it at her. "Any last words?"

A shadow appeared at the door. It was a masked man. He as well held a gun. "You! Say your last words!"

Pauline looked up from her crouched position and smiled. Simon had arrived late, but not too late. She had sent a message to him through Ben and explained everything to him. She knew Simon wanted to repay blood with blood. He wasn't interested in getting Robert arrested. He had lost a sister, his only family. To him, justice was the death of Robert.

But for Pauline, she was no better if she let such a thing happen. The evidence against him was overwhelming, and she had thought he would surely go to prison. A bit of her had hoped he would turn himself in, and that he would be remorseful, but now she knew that perhaps Simon was right in his thinking. Perhaps her husband needed to die. Perhaps in death, he would find the validation he had been seeking.

Rob turned around surprised. He looked at the man then back at Pauline. Who was the intruder, he wondered. Before he could swing the gun at the intruder, Simon pulled the trigger. Robert screamed as the bullet pierced his left shoulder. He had never felt such pain in his entire life. He fell to the ground and dropped the gun.

"This is revenge on behalf of my sister, Janet," Simon said, moving closer to him. "I have failed her before and I won't again. You killed her, bastard, you're not going to live."

As he cocked the gun again to finish what he had started, Pauline curled herself with her ears covered. Simon pointed the gun at Robert ready to shoot. Then he froze at the footsteps at the door.

The door was pushed hard, almost removing it from its hinges. "This is the police!" a voice yelled. "Drop your weapon or we will shoot you!"

Simon could feel the tears fill his eyes. He had failed his sister. He wanted the bastard dead. He heard the warning of the police again and dropped his weapon. Immediately, he was pushed hard against a wall and was handcuffed with his mask pulled from his head.

"Help me!!" Robert cried clutching his shoulder. He slowly made his way to the bed to get the phone before attention could be called to it. However, a hand picked it up before he could get to it. It was an officer. "Arrest him as well!!" the man said.

"No, you have got this all wrong. I am the victim here. I was shot! Look at my shoulder. Look at my arm!" Robert yelled.

"Give him medical attention first, then take him to the station," Officer John said.

"Do you know who I am?!" Robert spat.

"Yes," Officer John said. "You're a murderer. We have it all on tape. Take him away." He nodded at the policeman holding him. "I need medical help here," he called as he rushed to Pauline. "Are you okay madam?" he asked.

Pauline nodded. She had a terrible headache and her body hurt really badly, but yes she was perfectly fine. The monster had been gotten hold of. "What took you so long?" she asked.

"I'm sorry Ma for not believing in you when you came around. These things are delicate. They…"

Pauline waved him off. What mattered now was that her husband had been revealed for the murderer he was and had been apprehended. She closed her eyes and took a breath of relief.

*

7 days later

Pauline shook her head as Robert continued to complain that he was still not medically fit. For a week he had been holding on to that to avoid being taken away by the police, but the doctors had given him a clean bill of health and even though he whined, the police were going to take him away. It was time for him to dance to the tune of the music played by him.

Pauline herself had gone through more of a series of treatment than she had imagined possible. Robert had hurt her physically and it had taken her a while to recover. She was glad to be heading home in good shape.

"Look, we need to take you to the station, you cannot avoid this anymore," one of the officers said.

"But I am still not fit," Robert complained.

The handcuffs were slammed onto his hands and he was led away with Pauline following behind. She could see the glares he threw at her, but she did not care. He could not hurt her anymore. As a matter of fact, he could not hurt anyone anymore. He was going to where he rightfully belonged, behind bars. As for Simon, he had a good lawyer who had got him out on bail. Hopefully, he was going to walk away from jail time.

When they got out of the hospital, she froze. The press were outside of the police. For days following the incident, she had been receiving phone calls from friends and distant family. Even those who knew her closely had no idea of the ordeal she had been going through. To all of them, Robert had been a lively and caring man. That was the way with people like him were, they acted like they were sane to the public and meanwhile they were wicked on the inside. People were still trying to come to terms with it, but she knew she had no explanation to give them.

"Mr. Smith, what do you have to say to the press? Mr. Smith?" a reporter called.

Robert only glared at them. He was shoved into the police car which drove away. However, they made sure to take several pictures of him before the car drove away. She knew he would be staying there for a while. According to Officer John, he had been refused bail by the judge, and it was going to remain that way.

The reporters from UTR daily news and PHG surrounded her to get some words from her. A reporter pushed a microphone at her. "Mrs. Smith, this is Mama Abena Serwaa Sarpong of UTR daily news. We have heard different versions of what happened that night. Please tell us what truly happened."

Pauline smiled. "Today is a great day for women's liberation in this country. My mom said to me when I was young, 'Pauline, I pray to God that one day, women shall be liberated from abusive relationships and marriages. I pray to God that he gives you the strength to carry out the advocacy work I could not do...'"

EPILOGUE

"I never knew this happened to you," Joyce said. "I mean, I heard about this story in the news but I never knew you were the woman involved."

Pauline smiled. "Some of us keep our battles quiet. It was an ordeal for me, but I have moved past it."

"And how has it been? How do you cope? Do you regret anything you did?"

Pauline shook her head. "I don't. I only wish I had come out of that trauma I was in from that ordeal sooner. There are too many women in this country who are suffering from domestic abuse. Being assaulted by your husband is considered a social norm. Evil has become normal and is being accepted.

These women are too scared to come out in public. Too scared about what people will say. Do you know the names my in-laws still call me? They say I am responsible for their son being sentenced to 20 years imprisonment. They call me a witch, crazy woman and all sort of names. When I filed for a divorce and was given the house, they came to the house ready to push me out, but I stood my ground. The women are blamed for being beaten. The first question asked is what did you do? They don't care to know that there are sick people out there who get delighted by preying on those weaker than them."

Joyce nodded. "I once told my in-law and he asked me what I did. I tried to tell him that I did nothing wrong and he said there must be something that I am doing wrong."

Pauline laughed. "How many men are willing to stand up against another man and fight him because he did something wrong to him? They would rather walk away from a fight because they know there's the probability that they will be beaten up. You see several men walking away from a fight but when it comes to confrontations with women, they are quick to flex their muscles and beat them up in an attempt to correct them.

But that era is over; it is the time to educate women on their rights. To make them aware that no one should treat them like less than human beings. Too many times women are scared of what's out there. It is better to leave a violent husband than die and live in emotional misery."

"So what's going to happen to me now?" Joyce asked.

"You're going to think this over and decide what's best for you and what's best for your children's future. Remember, you're not alone. You need to do what's best for you and not what people will say. There's a lot of support out there my sister. I thought I was alone until I emerged out of that broken marriage. Then I discovered a sisterhood of love. Everything is going to be okay."

Joyce nodded wiping tears off her face. "Thank you, my sister."

Pauline looked up at the sky with tears in her eyes. She had gone through some counselling to regain and strengthen her self-esteem and she was happy that she had discovered herself. She was a strong and confident woman ready to fight for her suffering sisters.

"Mama," Pauline said. "Can you hear me? I hope you can. I want you to know that your dream has come true. I want you to know that I am free. You have helped me all this while and I fed from your strength. Thank you, mama, for believing in me and for making me the strong woman that I am today. *Mida wasia ensa daa…*"

18435954R00079

Printed in Poland
by Amazon Fulfillment
Poland Sp. z o.o., Wrocław